THE CLUB

CORNELIUS MOORE

ISBN: 1533189463
ISBN 13: 9781533189462
Library of Congress Control Number: 2016908129
CreateSpace Independent Publishing Platform
North Charleston, South Carolina

CHAPTER 1

Katherine walks out of her sprawling colonial-style home, looks up at the crystal-blue sky, closes her eyes to bask in the warm sun, and then opens her eyes and thinks, What a wonderful day for a funeral. Of course, she would never say that out loud because it would be inappropriate. She learned that lesson some time ago—unlike her husband, who still says things he should not say. Wearing a simple black dress, dark glasses, and a stylish wide-brimmed black hat, and with the gentle, brisk breeze from the east flowing through her silky blond hair, she looks like a model waiting for a photo shoot to begin. Today would have been the perfect day to hang out at the club, have a nice drink, and just relax. But duty calls, in a manner of speaking. Katherine is still a stunner at thirty-one years old, with piercing blue eyes and standing five foot ten.

A few minutes later, her husband, Edwyn, comes outside and checks his watch twice in thirty seconds. He then adjusts the sleeve on his black suit. Edwyn is in his late sixties and is as vain now as he was when he was in his early thirties. When he was a young man, you could clearly tell he was a lady-killer. In fact, there's a very well-known story about when he was a younger man and walked into the Russian Tea Room alone and walked out with three women. But that was then, and this is now. Although he does have more than a few lines on his face, he is still strikingly handsome. He still has a full head of salt-and-pepper hair and perfectly straight, white teeth. At this age, he still turns the heads of women of all ages, colors, and creeds. He likes to think of his sexual prowess with women as comparable to that of former President Bill

Clinton. That is the second-term Bill Clinton, not the first-term one. His hair was much grayer after the stress from his first term, and it showed. He was four years older, wiser, and, in the opinion of many women the world over, much better looking. Women couldn't keep their hands and mouths off his cock, and he was more than willing to oblige. But one of the things Edwyn is proudest of is his name. Edwyn was named after his father, who was named after his father. And it's Edwyn: E-D-W-Y-N. It means wealthy or rich friend, and, since birth, that name has given him a self-proclaimed sense of entitlement. And he likes to be called Edwyn—not Edwin, Eddie, Ed, or Edward. He hates when people do not refer to him by his given name, and he refuses to shorten it, abbreviate it, or allow people to use a nickname.

Edwyn checks his watch again. "Where are they?" he says impatiently.

"They will be here," Katherine responds without looking at him.

"I thought she was supposed to be here at ten."

"She was, but we cut her hours."

"Why'd we do that?"

Now Katherine turns to look at him and says, "Because we couldn't afford to keep her full time."

Edwyn looks at her as if the lights have just come on. Just then, a Maserati Quattro Porto pulls up to the house, and out come Ernesto and Eugenia. Katherine has a slight look of relief on her face, while Edwyn's expression shows more contempt for the car Ernesto is driving.

"Sorry we're late, Miss Katherine. We had to make a stop," Eugenia says very apologetically.

"No worries. The funeral doesn't start until ten. Come with me into the kitchen so I can show you a few things," Katherine says.

She leads Eugenia to the kitchen while Edwyn is still looking at the Maserati. He moves toward his own Lexus to try to show his status in the neighborhood. "You need to move your car," Edwyn says, his voice dripping with disdain.

"And I will as soon as Eugenia comes out. The funeral isn't until ten, remember?" replies Ernesto, who clearly hears the disapproval with a slight tinge of disgust in Edwyn's voice.

"How is a guy like you able to afford a car like this?" asks Edwyn, who is basing his question on Ernesto's Asian facial features but can't quite place his country of origin as he wonders, He's too dark to be Chinese, too tall to be Japanese, and what is that accent? But he's definitely from somewhere over there. Edwyn tries to remember how many countries are in Asia. A lot, he guesses.

"The same way a guy like you can afford a house like this," says Ernesto coldly, obviously taking Edwyn for a WASP who feels only people like him deserve to drive a car like that. "I make my money the same way you do. Or the way you used to," Ernesto adds for good measure.

Not being smart enough to come up with a reply, Edwyn mumbles under his breath, "I doubt that."

Inside the house, the sprawling remodeled kitchen, with its huge wood cabinets, large island, and double ovens, almost seems to swallow Katherine and Eugenia as they stand in the wide-open space. The room could fit twenty people without them bumping into one another. The women stand in front of the refrigerator looking at the grocery list on the electronic screen. Eugenia reads, "Pick up the dry cleaning. Get eggs and milk. While at the market, should I—"

"Where's that five thousand dollars I gave your brother?" interrupts Katherine, whose face now shows a bit more agitation.

"There was a problem, but it's been corrected," Eugenia says in a soothing voice.

"And what the fuck does that mean? 'I can double your money. I guarantee it.' Isn't that what he told me? Weren't those his exact words?" Katherine raises her voice ever so slightly. "Edwyn has no idea I gave you the money, and I want to keep it that way. You need to give me a firm date when I'll get this money back, because I don't want to fuck this up. I can't fuck this up."

"Tomorrow, I promise," Eugenia says, putting her hand on Katherine's shoulder for reassurance.

Katherine slides her hand off, saying, "I don't believe in promises anymore." Her voice trails off. She is well aware of the validity of promises now, most of which are empty.

Katherine and Eugenia go back outside to hear Edwyn inquire about the cost of the car. Ernesto's response is muffled but is somewhere along the lines of, "If you have to ask the question, you can't afford the answer." Upon seeing Eugenia, Ernesto gives a thumbs-up. Eugenia replies with a thumbs-up, and with that, Ernesto gets in his car and takes off down the road.

"What does your brother do again, Eugenia?" Katherine asks.

"He's a human-resources manager," she replies and walks back into the house before a follow-up question can be asked.

"How can he afford a car like that as an HR manager?" asks Edwyn, but Eugenia has already slipped into the house and pretended not to hear. Katherine gives Edwyn a disapproving look and ushers him into the car so they can be on their way.

In the car, Edwyn is driving, and Katherine is throwing daggers at him with her eyes. Yes, she is also curious about how Ernesto makes his money, but she thinks there might have been a better way to ask. "You really should be careful about some of the things you say," Katherine says, looking at him and waiting for a response. But his mind seems to be elsewhere.

"I wonder how much she'll get," Edwyn mumbles.

Clearly his mind is elsewhere. He probably didn't hear the question, Katherine thinks. She contemplates asking if he was listening.

"You ever wondered about that? How much Arlene will get?" Edwyn asks again. He seems so fixated on figuring out who is making what and how much.

"Listen, you have to promise you will not ask her about that," Katherine says sternly, looking him right in the eye.

Edwyn glances into her eyes and says, "Why not?"

As she sucks her teeth and rolls her eyes, he can feel it in his pores. "Listen—" Katherine says before being cut off by her husband.

"The old man had real estate, horse farms, stocks, bonds, and an oil field in Texas. She was an only child, so it all goes to her," Edwyn says with a slight smile on his face.

"Brett told you all that?" Katherine asks.

"Yeah. How'd you know Brett told me?"

4

Katherine doesn't answer, but she knows that since Arlene hates his guts and can't stand the very sight of him, there is no way in hell she would have told him. Arlene's father is dead and only knew Edwyn in passing and wasn't crazy about him. Brett seems like the logical choice—the only choice, when you think about it.

"Please don't mention that to anybody, least of all her. Not on the day she's burying her father. Can you at least promise me that?" Katherine almost sounds as if she begging.

"Lucky bastard," he says almost with disdain.

"Arlene?" She raises her voice.

"No, Brett." He raises his voice also. He hates being yelled at.

Katherine finally has had enough and desperately wants to change the subject. "You know, we still haven't gotten our check yet from Bernie," she says as her voice now comes back to a normal level.

"I know. I left several messages, but he should be there today."

When they arrive at the church, they see many cars outside already. The hearse is sitting right in front, with the driver leaning against it smoking a cigarette. It's obvious they're late. Katherine checks her watch.

"Shit, they've already started. We should have left earlier," Katherine says.

"We'll be fine. We'll just have to sneak in. No one will notice us," Edwyn says, almost with an air of arrogance. They walk up to the massive church door, and Katherine tries to open it. As she struggles with it, she tries in vain to get the attention of Edwyn, who is busy watching people walk by. He finally turns around to give his wife some much-needed aid. The two of them are able to open the door just enough for Edwyn to slip through. He tries to hold the door open long enough for Katherine to enter, which she does, but not before the door slams shut with such force that everyone in the church feels the tailwind. Needless to say, everyone in attendance—close friends, the priest, and the grieving family—must now pause in their bereavement to see where this sudden gust of wind is coming from. This includes Arlene and Brett Kinney, the daughter and son-in-law of the deceased. She looks up at Edwyn, appalled, trying not to believe Edwyn is vying for attention at someone else's funeral. Brett looks more embarrassed than angry. As everyone stops to look at them, Katherine gives Edwyn a gaze of disgust. Instead of Edwyn being completely embarrassed by what he has done, he takes pride in people looking at him and gives a smile and a slight wave. But now, instead of sitting closer to the front as they wanted, they will have to settle for sitting in the back pew.

At the cemetery, many family members and friends of the deceased file past the casket, each placing a single red rose on top of it. Finally, the priest signals for Arlene to come forward. Most of the crowd steps back a little to give her grieving room. While Arlene is not known for public displays of affection, most of the mourners have figured she will now really let loose emotionally—hopefully nothing too dramatic such as wailing, screaming, and finally jumping into the hole where her loved one is buried while shouting, "Take me with you!" After all, it's not every day you bury your father and last parent. Instead, she barely looks at the coffin and flings the rose in its general direction.

People approach her and Brett to offer their condolences. Edwyn walks up to Brett and gives him a strong, solid hug. They have known each other ever since the college jobs fair. "Hey, I'm so sorry for your loss. I know you were close to your father-in-law," Edwyn says.

"Thanks, buddy. I really appreciate it." Brett starts to move away, but Edwyn steps slightly in front of him and moves a little closer.

"Out of curiosity, have you seen Bernie?" Edwyn says, almost as an afterthought.

Katherine cuts her eyes at him, knowing full well it's much more than an afterthought.

"No. He called to say he couldn't make it. Something big came up," Brett replies as he politely yet firmly moves Edwyn out of the way. He also gives Edwyn a second glance, possibly realizing what he's getting at.

Katherine greets Arlene with a warm hug and a peck on the cheek. "I wish I had the words," Katherine says while rubbing Arlene's back.

"Me too," Arlene replies. She has always kept her cards close to her chest. You never quite understand what she means when she says certain things. Katherine gives Brett a warm condolence hug as well. As Edwyn moves toward Arlene, you can already see her tense up. He tries to put his arms around her, but she places her hands in front of her, almost to block him.

"I'm so sorry for your loss," Edwyn says.

"I know, Eddie," Arlene replies with a slight smile. He moves in to give her a kiss, but she turns her face and screws her mouth so far he practically has to kiss her on her lower jaw.

"You know I don't like when people call me that," Edwyn says with a forced chuckle.

"I know, Eddie," Arlene replies with an even louder chuckle. She looks Edwyn right in the eyes and then rolls her eyes, pushes him off, moves toward Katherine, and says, "You ready?"

Katherine is a little confused. "Right now?" she says. "I know you said you wanted to wait until—"

Arlene grabs her by the hand and squeezes tight and says, "No. I'm ready now." Arlene gathers her purse, swings it across her shoulders, and marches toward the limo that brought her to the funeral. Katherine turns to Edwyn and Brett and says, "OK, then. Brett, I'm kidnapping your wife for a few hours. Don't wait up."

"Don't worry," Brett replies. "We'll be at the club if you need us."

Katherine gives Edwyn a peck on the lips, while Brett gives Arlene a long hug and a kiss. The crowd starts to disperse as Katherine and Arlene slip into the limo and it slowly drives away. Brett and Edwyn take Edwyn's car back to the club. As the last of the cars pull out, the cemetery foreman gives the sign, and the crew starts the process of lowering the casket into the ground and then covering it up with earth.

⋏

Raffaele opened his hair salon shortly after he'd saved enough money working as a chef for an Italian restaurant on the Lower East Side. He was actually a very talented chef, cooking up recipes from the southern town of Avellino, where he grew up. He would always recall the day he decided to leave and the manager, Antonio, begged him to stay. He says the man was down on his hands and knees pleading, "Without-a you, my-a restaurant-a will-a fail!"

"I'm-a sorry, Anton," Raffaele said with a stern look. And without uttering another word, he left and never looked back. Cooking was his joy, but hair was his passion. He had all the legends there—Jackie O, who was a great tipper, and Leona Helmsley, who never tipped at all. She felt his rates were too high. Many stars of stage and screen frequented his shop as well. But, as the saying goes, all good things must come to an end. First Jackie O died, and then Leona went to jail and eventually died. Little by little revenue started to drop off. Raffaele was also a savvy businessman and recognized the signs of an economic downturn and adjusted accordingly, which is why he's still in business and his major and minor competitors have all gone bankrupt.

Arlene has been going to him since she was a little girl. She always liked the way Raffaele would dote on her and make her look far more mature than she actually was. Raffaele has since retired from the hairstyling business. But he passed all of his skills on to the other stylists. The one who really is the most talented and mirrors Raffaele's motions is Gary, which makes sense because he's been with Raffaele the longest.

Arlene and Katherine arrive shortly after leaving the cemetery. As he tenderly cuts Arlene's long, flowing locks of auburn hair, Gary thinks of himself as not just cutting her hair but also as healing her from a difficult time. He turns her around in the chair to show the finished product, and Arlene is amazed at how different she looks, even though she still has the same face. She produces her first real smile of the day. "Gary, you are amazing."

Gary touches her hair. "Girl, don't I know it."

She hands him some money and closes his fist. "How can I thank you for such a wonderful job?"

Gary looks down at his hand, which holds a $500 tip. "This is one way to start!"

Arlene gives him a big hug. Katherine comes over, also with her hair in a new style. Following her is Annie, the stylist who did Katherine's hair. She stands next to Arlene, and the two women compliment and touch each other's hair like little girls at a sleepover. Gary joins the fray, offering humorous anecdotes and making everyone laugh, especially Arlene. For a short while, everything—from the issues with money to the funeral to the future—is forgotten.

Gary signals Raffaele to come over. Raffaele is well aware of the funeral Arlene attended and wants to make sure she's been taken care of. The staff is responsible for making the mood as light as possible. Gary in particular is supposed to make Arlene laugh and forget most of the funeral. Once Gary had Arlene laughing loudly, Raffaele knew that was his moment to enter.

Upon seeing him, Arlene stops laughing only slightly, to give him a huge bear hug. All of the employees clap and cheer. The mood has never been better. "How are you, *bella*?" Raffaele says with his remaining slight Italian accent.

"I'm OK," Arlene replies, with a smile still on her face.

"I'm sorry for your loss. I knew your dad well. He came here a lot," Raffaele says.

"I know," Arlene replies, dropping her smile. "He'd bring his girlfriends here quite often. Later, my mother would ask you if you'd seen my dad, and you always lied for him."

And with those few short sentences, the mood dies down like the air being choked out of a balloon, whereas before it was so festive you could probably have said anything you wanted, however inappropriate, because everyone was in a good mood. Now, no one wants to move, let alone speak. Raffaele is not sure how to respond, so he glances at Gary, who now only wants to crawl under the nearest table.

Raffaele makes eye contact with Katherine, who seems just as eager as he is to change the subject. "Katherine, you look as lovely as ever. It's been a while since I saw you last. How long has it been? Two months?" he says with slight desperation, hoping Katherine will take the hint.

"Yes. It has been a while," she says as Raffaele lets out a silent sigh. "I was thinking about going natural for a change."

"Really?" Raffaele says, wanting to stay on topic.

"Yeah, I'm thinking about it. But I haven't made a decision yet. But when I do—"

Arlene steps slightly in between the two of them to show she is not interested in what they are talking about and is now ready to leave altogether. "Anyway, you ready to go, Kat?" she says.

Katherine looks at her calmly to gauge her mood and quickly says, "Sure, let's go," while gathering up her belongings.

Arlene shoots Raffaele a slight look indicating she is aware of his subject-changing tactic before kissing him on the cheek. "I'll talk to you later, Raffaele."

He gives her a sheepish look and kisses her back.

Katherine gives him a kiss as well and says, "I'll let you know what I decide to do."

"Whatever you decide, we will be here, my dear," Raffaele says to her.

Both ladies give the staff a big wave and leave.

Raffaele gathers his staff around him for an impromptu meeting. "We live in very hard economic times, people," he says with much reflection.

Annie looks at the fifty-dollar tip Katherine gave her, which is not very impressive. "You ain't kidding," she says with reserved sarcasm.

"How can you tell?" Gary asks with slight confusion.

Raffaele speaks now as if he is a professor. "Katherine used to come in here every six weeks, and now she comes in every two months and is thinking of going natural? Really? Who are these people kidding? She's watching what she's spending. You pick up on these subtle hints very quickly. People like that don't beg."

"What happened to her?" Gary asks.

"Katherine's husband was a bigwig at an investment firm. He was making a shitload of money. Then he got laid off, but he likes to refer to it as a buyout. He's very sensitive about that, actually."

Annie moves closer to Raffaele and asks, "How long ago did he lose his job?"

"Almost two years ago," Raffaele says. And with those words, the staff watches Arlene and Katherine drive away as they absorb the lesson they have just learned on how trickle-down economics can directly affect their pockets.

CHAPTER 2

Reginald Archibald Daniels, or Archie, as he was called, was a man who could never have too much of a good thing. Already a legend in his native England because of his trading-goods business, he opened his first shop to much fanfare on 149th Street and Third Avenue in the Bronx on March 2, 1890. Archie only had four main items to sell: tea, coffee, sugar, and flour. People came from all five boroughs, New Jersey, Westchester County, and Connecticut for his products. One day, an architect named Albert Simonsen arrived at his store with his two young daughters, fifteen-year-old Penelope and six-year-old Virginia, to inquire about purchasing some goods even though he didn't have much money. Archie took one look at Penelope and was smitten. He told Albert they would work something out. He swept Penelope off her feet with fancy dinners, outings to the ballet, and trips around the world. They married in April 1891 and, as a wedding gift, Albert designed the finest house he could. He called it a house, but it was more like a mansion. It was a four-level, twelve-bedroom, 12,510-square-foot structure that at the time dwarfed the other houses in Westchester County. The home was made with the finest materials, such as marble, stone, and mahogany. Each room had a particular style, theme, and color that flowed like a classic painting. The large living room had double doors that opened out into a large living space big enough for a dining room table with twelve chairs. Albert's intention was to create a loving environment for his daughter and new son-in-law. And for many years, it was. He had accounted for every detail in the house except one: Archie always had a roving eye, and this house gave him the perfect opportunity to do pretty much what he wanted. He would have a paramour in one part of the house and his wife in the next. Penelope was always tolerant of his adulterous ways because she loved the lifestyle Archie provided.

One day when she was about to go out, she heard Archie coming in with yet another conquest. She heard them come upstairs toward the bedroom, so Penelope hid in a hallway closet. Once they went into the bedroom and began making love, Penelope moved closer. She recognized the female voice but couldn't believe it until she opened the bedroom door to confirm. There was her little sister, Virginia, who was not so little at almost seventeen years old, naked with her brother-in-law, having wild and passionate sex in the bed where she and her husband slept. They were so caught up in their own passion, they never noticed Penelope as she stood over them. She was in shock at this sight and knew at that moment what had to be done.

She went to Archie's private study, opened the gun case, and took out his favorite Colt pistol. She checked that it was loaded, and, as she made her way back upstairs, she was thankful her dear father was dead. What she was about to do would have killed him! Archie never heard Penelope when she walked up behind him, never heard her when she cocked the gun, and never heard her when she pulled the trigger.

As soon as Archie's his body went limp, Victoria jerked forward. She looked up long enough to see her sister pointing the gun at her head. Victoria barely had time to plead for her life before Penelope pulled the trigger. She stared at the two bodies now that only a few moments ago had been gyrating in unison like the beast with two backs of old and pondered what to do next. She went downstairs to the basement where the extra cans of kerosene were kept and started pouring gasoline everywhere—all over the kitchen, the bathroom, all the bedrooms, and especially the master bedroom. As she lit a match, she thought back on all the hard work her father had put into the house and how he had wanted nothing but joy and happiness. But then, looking at the naked bodies of her husband and sister, she realized the house could never stand again. She threw the match against the door and lay between Archie and Victoria.

The thick black cloud of smoke could be seen for miles around. Apparently as a result of the kind of materials used to build the house, it took the fire department six hours to get the fire under control and another eight to put it completely out. The scandal made the front page for weeks afterward, with new details emerging every day. But eventually, like the fire itself, the story died down and was forgotten about. The effects however, were still felt.

For many years after the incident, the house lay in rubble. No one wanted to go near it because the house was considered bad luck. Then rumors started to surface about Penelope's ghost causing children to disappear in the house. In fact, the police had the place searched twice because neighbors swore they heard children screaming from inside.

The house was finally bricked up for good, and it stayed that way for many years until 1971, when some of the local well-to-doers thought enough was enough, that this place was too much of an eyesore. It was also bringing down the property values of all the surrounding homes, which was a huge problem. These men decided to take equal shares to buy the house from the county, fix it up, and use it as a gentlemen's club. Total renovations were completed in 1975, and the Club for Westchester Men was established.

Pretty soon, many prominent people in the area wanted to get in. The founders decided to set the maximum number of members admitted at twenty-five, no exceptions. The only way a new member would be admitted was when an old member died. Even if a member moved out of the state or the country, or even went to jail, his membership would still be valid if he decided to move back or was released from jail. The club had only three rules. Granted, these were unwritten rules that everyone knew but no one mentioned—ever. They were mainly there because the members could get sued and have the club shut down. But as a result of these rules and the way they were implemented, the founding members could be very selective in their membership and deny applicants for any reason.

Edwyn Collingsworth was admitted as a member in 1982, but only after a personal phone call from the firm's CEO, who also happened to be a member. There was a rumor that Katherine told certain people that Edwyn actually got sexually aroused and had an erection for five hours when he got the call that his membership had been approved.

Brett became a member because of the sudden death of a previous member. Some thought it was cold and impersonal for Edwyn to nominate someone so soon afterward. But, as it turned out, because Brett was sponsored by Edwyn, his application went through rather smoothly.

Wives weren't allowed, but there were special days when spouses could have access to the pool, firing range, and bar. The club members were able to be selective with the hired staff as well. They wanted to hire people who would perform a variety of duties and be very discreet about it, such as acquiring drugs and women. One of the people whom Edwyn desperately wanted to hire was a man named Jabari Douglas Sr.

Jabari Sr. started out as a messenger for the financial firm Edwyn worked for and became a valuable resource, so much so that Edwyn used him for "special projects," for which he was given additional pay upon completion of each assignment. His sudden and accidental death left Edwyn devastated. Out of respect and loyalty for Jabari Sr., Edwyn wanted Jabari Jr. to take his father's place at the club. Although Jabari Jr. was a good worker, he didn't share Edwyn's enthusiasm or affinity for special projects.

⅄

Tonight, many of the members are doing what they usually do: smoking, drinking, and screwing women other than their wives, but mainly patting one another on the back for their achievements as the kings of all creation. They are all high-ranking players, wheelers and dealers in their areas of expertise, whether it is finance, art, medicine, or law. There is nothing better than working hard all day, coming to the club at night, and congratulating one another on having large dicks that other peons would envy. They feel noble. They feel as though they are the ones who keep the economy going and create jobs to give the lower and the middle class something to believe in and strive for. In fact, they want to be looked up to as a measure of wealth and prosperity, and if the lower classes work hard and really apply themselves, they might achieve that level of success. This, of course, will never really happen because the lower classes will only be allowed to make a certain amount of money each year. It is the never-ending catch-22: give them enough to dream, but not enough to see that dream become a reality. But, as the old saying goes, what good is it to be rich if you don't have poor people to kick around?

On this night, Edwyn and Brett are in the outdoor living space, enjoying the crisp air and reflecting on the events of the day. Edwyn notices Brett's sad expression and tries to cheer him up. He grabs the shotgun used for skeet shooting and says, "Hey, you wanna pop some off?"

Brett looks at the shotgun, smiles slightly, and says, "Not today. I'm really wiped. This has all been so stressful. And given that it's been so busy at work, that doesn't really help much."

This catches Edwyn's interest. He presses but tries not to make it seem as if he's that interested. "Really? What's going on?" he asks.

"We have a lot of new projects happening right now and not enough manpower. George has been going out to so many meetings recently and spending so much time outside of the office, we are swamped. What we need is more staff. You should call George and ask him if he could use your help," Brett replies.

Before Edwyn can say anything, Brett hands him his cell phone. "Leave him a message."

Edwyn stares at the phone for a second.

Meanwhile, Jabari Jr. is inside, moving through the thick cloud of cigars, cigarettes, and egos with two drinks in his hand, working his way to where Edwyn and Brett are seated. He passes Leonard, a blond, pimply twenty-something who also works there. As Jabari passes him, Leonard sticks his foot out and tries to trip him. He almost succeeds, but Jabari regains his footing. Leonard gives him a slight smile. "You need to be more careful, brother."

Jabari cuts his eyes at Leonard but says nothing. Instead, he makes his way outside just in time to hear the tail end of Edwyn's message to George.

"Gentlemen, here are your drinks," Jabari says as he hands the drinks to their owners.

Despite Jabari's low-level status at the club, he and Brett have a lot of mutual respect for each other, as evidenced when Jabari extends his hand in condolence. "I heard about your father-in-law, Brett. I'm very sorry for your loss."

Brett gives him a firm, heartfelt handshake and says, "Thanks a lot, Jabari. I really appreciate that."

"It's always hard losing a father," Jabari says, while glancing at Edwyn and then quickly focusing back to Brett. Brett catches that glance and looks directly at Edwyn. Edwyn is thinking, Must divert attention now.

"You know, Jabari Sr. used to work for me also," Edwyn says as a little dig and twist of the knife.

Jabari turns to him and says with clarity, "He worked for the club, not you."

Brett has to muffle his laughter.

Again, Edwyn tries to change the subject. "That reminds me, JJ: before you came over, Brett was telling me how he needed to move some computer equipment out of his house. I told him we'd give him a hand."

Brett rolls his eyes with embarrassment and says, "If it's not too much trouble."

Edwyn comes over and stands next to Jabari. "It's not a problem at all. Right, JJ?"

"Don't call me JJ, Eddie," Jabari says in a serious tone.

"You know I hate it when people call me that," Edwyn says, changing his tone from a jovial ribbing to dead serious.

"Then don't call me JJ unless Buffalo Butt comes over. If he does, then it's a party," Jabari says with a straight face, knowing full well Edwyn has no idea what he's talking about. Edwyn wouldn't even know that JJ was a character in the old seventies sitcom *Good Times*. He would never lower himself by watching a show about an inner-city family from Chicago. Brett, however, is younger and grew up with very liberal parents who wanted to expose him to different things, and he thoroughly enjoyed various sitcoms from that era, including *Good Times*, *All in the Family*, *Maude*, and *Sanford and Son*. This is all evidenced by Jabari's giving Brett a wink before returning back inside.

Edwyn stands there lost as Brett chuckles a bit, unable to suppress his laughter or amusement. "I always liked Jabari," Brett says with admiration.

Edwyn rolls his eyes and says, "You have to be careful around those people."

Brett is very confused by that statement. "Those people?" he asks.

Edwyn moves closer to him and says, "We have allowed people like him to be a part of our world."

"Why? Having him serve us food and drinks?" Brett says with slight sarcasm.

Edwyn lights a cigar and says smugly, "He should consider it an honor and a privilege to serve us. Where else would he be able to literally rub elbows with the likes of us? To shake our hands and get a very small taste of the good life?"

Brett ponders what Edwyn has said, takes a deep breath, stares out into the night, and says, "And when was the last time Jabari shook your hand?"

Before Edwyn responds, he asks, "Did your father-in-law have any gold? Gold is always a good investment."

Brett looks confused and slightly annoyed at Edwyn and says, "Where did that come from? As a matter of fact, he—"

Before he can finish, he turns to see Jabari standing there. Edwyn also turns to face Jabari, who has a slightly less amused look on his face. He says, "You should come and see this."

⅄

Edwyn and Brett glance at each other and follow Jabari into the TV viewing room, where they and the rest of the members see Bernie Madoff being led to a police car in handcuffs, followed by throngs of media. No one really knows how much he stole in his Ponzi scheme. One report says tens of millions. They switch to another channel, where the amount is said to be closer to billions.

You would think they were watching the funeral of John Pierpont Morgan and were being cut out of the will. That's how quiet it is in the house—not just the room, but the whole house. Anywhere there's a television, the Bernie Madoff case bellows throughout the house.

While the members are visibly shaking, the staff is more relaxed. More than relaxed—once in a while they make eye contact with one another and wink or nod their heads, knowing that crime doesn't pay no matter who you are.

Brett also seems indifferent to the story. After watching the TV for a while, he turns to go back outside and says, almost as a throwaway line, "At least now I know why he didn't show up at the funeral." Brett leaves Edwyn standing there, and he's not sure what to do or say.

Someone yells out, "Fuck! I need to call my lawyer!" Edwyn is actually thinking the same thing but is too ashamed to say anything. He's more worried about what to tell Katherine when he gets home.

Chapter 3

Katherine has a slightly perplexed look on her face, while Edwyn looks more haggard. "But I don't understand. How much money did he take?" Katherine says, concerned.

"No one knows. Some say in the billions," Edwyn says in almost a hushed tone.

She moves closer to him and says, "We didn't lose that much, did we?" Edwyn doesn't answer, so she moves even closer. "Did we?" Katherine asks again more forcefully.

Edwyn seems almost afraid now. "I might have given him a little more," he says meekly.

Katherine, now leaning slightly forward with her arms crossed, says, "How much more did you give him?"

Edwyn takes a more defensive stance and says, "He said it was a sure thing."

"How much more?" Katherine says through gritted teeth.

Edwyn hems and haws as long as he can and finally says, "Almost all of it." Katherine's piercing blue eyes get wide, and Edwyn can almost feel his testicles crawling up his ass.

"And you didn't consult me?" Katherine says, reminding him of what a marriage is supposed to mean.

"You didn't marry me to be consulted," Edwyn responds, reminding her of why she had agreed to marry him in the first place.

"What do we do now?" Katherine looks around the house, scanning the walls. "We still have plenty of paintings we could sell."

Edwyn marches toward a painting in the dining hall that looks to be worth well over $150,000. "Absolutely not," he barks. "I told you—we can't sell anything anybody would notice. It has to be something small. What about that diamond ring I bought you last year? You never liked it anyway."

Katherine moves a little closer to Edwyn and says, "I cashed that in three months ago."

"Fuck!" Edwyn says through gritted teeth. They stare at each other and then at the walls, the floors, the clock, or anything that might give them an idea.

"Didn't Brett say the company was very busy?" Katherine asks.

"Yes, and I've already left George several messages," Edwyn says.

They are still thinking. Katherine notices the puffy eyes, furrowed brow, and dry skin on Edwyn's face and finally lets out a big sigh. "I could get a part-time job or something. No one has to know."

Edwyn stands up and gets very defensive. "Doing what? What kind of skills do you have? No offense, but the only thing you were ever good at was fucking." He catches himself just in time to realize that that probably wasn't the best thing to say to his young wife. He relaxes his body language and tone and says, "I apologize. That was out of line."

Katherine moves a little closer to him. "It's not like I haven't tried. You just haven't been *up* to the challenge," she says while looking at his privates. Edwyn's pride has been wounded, and she knows it. She remembers when he could get erect just by reading the *Wall Street Journal*.

Edwyn tries to let that comment roll off his cock. "I deserve that. We do need to come up with a plan, but for now, we'll take that five grand and put it in the bank first thing in the morning. At least we can start to earn some interest on it." He walks past her, gives her a kiss on the cheek, and goes upstairs.

Katherine stands there for a minute and gets the shivers. She knows if Eugenia doesn't come through on her promise of doubling the money, or at the very least giving back the five thousand, they will be closer to broke than they both care to be. Katherine has never been this fearful of the future before and is not sure how she will respond to it. She is about to see what she is really made of.

⋏

The next morning when Eugenia and Ernesto drive up to the Collingsworth house, Katherine has already been waiting outside for what seems like an hour. Eugenia looks very worried, while Ernesto is not fazed at all. "She looks pissed," Eugenia says with slight reservations.

"Relax. I can handle her," Ernesto says with the utmost confidence.

Katherine walks right over to them as they exit the car. "Where is it?" she demands.

Ernesto hands her an envelope filled with cash. "It's all there," he adds for good measure. Katherine fans through the cash quickly with her thumb and can tell the amount is only $5,000.

"I thought you said I could double my money. Remember that?" Katherine asks while standing a little closer to him. He shuts her up by taking out another envelope filled with money. Katherine is dumbfounded. She has gone from potentially having no money at all to $10,000 in two weeks.

"Any questions?" Ernesto asks with a slight smile on his face.

Before Katherine can say anything, Edwyn comes out of the house looking frazzled. He says, "Honey, I'm on my way to the bank, and I was looking for—"

She hands him one of the envelopes before he can finish. "I brought it out for you, darling," she adds for a little extra sweetness. He seems a bit confused by that. She gives him a kiss. "I'll see you later, sweetheart," she says as Edwyn makes eye contact with Ernesto.

"Ernesto," he says with contempt.

"Edwyn," Ernesto replies with an equal amount of contempt.

Edwyn gets in his car and drives off. Ernesto gives a nod to Katherine and a wave to his sister as he starts to get back in his car. Before he can drive away, though, Katherine walks in front of it, which surprises him. "You work for a private investment firm? I know most of them. Which one do you work for?" she asks.

"If I told you that, it wouldn't be private," Ernesto responds rather cryptically.

They stare at each other for a few minutes, sizing each other up. Katherine has never really thought much of Ernesto but now is very interested in knowing more about him and, more importantly, what he does for a living. Ernesto figured Katherine out shortly after Eugenia started working for them. They were stuck-up superficial suburban people living in a bubble who had no idea what was going on around them. His opinion hasn't changed.

"Take me there," she says finally.

"You want to come to my job? Not sure that's a good idea."

Katherine walks over to the passenger side of his car and puts her hand on the handle. "I'm not like my husband. I'm not as dumb as you think. I insist, and I won't take no for an answer," she says defiantly.

Ernesto gets out of the car and walks around to her side to get a good look at her face. He then looks at her up and down. This could be interesting. "Sure. Why not?"

As he unlocks her side and opens the door for her to get in, Eugenia has a worried look on her face. "Are you sure this is a good idea?" she asks, clearly not comfortable with this.

"She wants to see how real money is made. I will show her," Ernesto says as he gets in the car and tears off down the street.

⋏

As he drives, Ernesto periodically steals quick glances at Katherine's body. He takes particular interest in her legs. Katherine catches him, and he slowly looks away. She tries to feign annoyance but is still flattered when a man looks at her body, especially a man who drives a car like this. It makes her think she's still got it. "What do you think you're doing?" she asks, trying not to sound too obvious.

Ernesto looks at her body again. "What does it look like I'm doing? I'm checking you out. Your legs, your chest, and your ass—and I must say, you are very well put together," he says with the utmost confidence.

Katherine remains on the defensive. "Well, don't get any bright ideas," she says defiantly.

Ernesto glances at her again and slightly smiles. "Bright ideas are some of the reasons why I'm driving this car."

Katherine can't help but admire his confidence. It reminds her of how Edwyn used to be.

The car pulls up to a large but fairly simple-looking house, the last on a dead-end street in the Bronx. As the car stops, Ernesto notices Wendell standing outside. He looks a little nervous and keeps looking over his shoulder, as if he is expecting someone to meet him there.

Ernesto looks extremely annoyed at seeing Wendell there. "Shit. Wait here," he commands Katherine as he gets out of the car and slams the door. Wendell is a large and imposing man, about six feet tall and almost 220 pounds. Conversely, Ernesto is about five foot six and almost 200 pounds. It might seem like a mismatch, but Ernesto is quite resilient when he needs to be.

"I told you not to come here," Ernesto says with fervor.

Wendell moves a little closer to him. "I'm trying to be civil about this," he says in almost a whisper. He then looks Ernesto right in the eyes and tries to intimidate him.

Ernesto sees this and responds in kind. "I know what you do for a living, and I'm not afraid of you," Ernesto says.

"I know what you do for a living, and you should be afraid of me," Wendell says.

"Was that a threat?"

At this point Wendell pulls out a gun, and while he doesn't point it at Ernesto, the fact that a weapon is in the air makes the conversation much tenser.

Katherine, who has been watching the exchange from the car and can't make out everything that has been said, sees the gun. She immediately sits up. "Oh, shit!" she exclaims.

Meanwhile, Wendell is still staring at Ernesto, waiting for him to blink. "Would you like for me to threaten you?" he asks with a slight smile.

Ernesto takes a slight step back and says, "What are you going to do? Take me down? What about everybody in the house? What about the cameras? Do you really want to do this in broad daylight? You need to get the fuck out of here before I call a real cop."

The smile that was on Wendell's face fades away as he slowly backs up, returns the gun to his pocket, and walks away.

Once Wendell is a safe distance away, Ernesto motions for Katherine to get out of the car.

"A real cop?" Katherine asks.

"Never mind that. Let's go."

⋀

As they make their way to the front door, Katherine takes a look at the house, which is a modest-looking stand-alone two-story. "You own this house?" she asks.

"I do. There was a murder-suicide years ago when some dude was fucking around on his wife. She killed him and then set the house on fire. It was boarded up and abandoned for years. I loved the location because it was out of the way, so I bought it off the city, and they were more than happy to get rid of it. I got it for close to nothing. I fixed it up, and here it is," Ernesto says in almost a tour-guide-like way.

Katherine looks at the house again and chuckles to herself, considering how the Westchester Club came to be.

"What's so funny?" he asks.

"History does repeat himself," she says.

They reach the front of the house, and Ernesto stands facing the security camera and gets buzzed in. Inside, right off the front door at the reception desk, sits Amelia, a very attractive Filipino girl wearing an extremely sexy nightgown and high heels. Katherine looks around the first level of the house and sees many other scantily clad Filipino girls, and, following behind them like dogs chasing treats are middle-aged white men wearing suits that must have cost several thousand dollars.

Ernesto approaches Amelia, who greets him with a generous kiss on the lips. "Any issues?" he asks while he sifts through the mail.

"So far, so good," Amelia says. She then turns her attention to Katherine, gives her the once-over, and asks, "New client?"

Ernesto smiles slightly while looking Katherine up and down and says, "Secret investor. She wants to see how real money is made."

Amelia looks at Katherine again, who seems very much like a deer in the headlights during this whole encounter.

"We'll be in my office," Ernesto says, and they walk toward his office, which used to be one of the first-floor bedrooms. As Katherine follows Ernesto, she sees a man middle-aged man wearing nothing but a T-shirt and underwear chasing a young girl down the staircase, waving an eggbeater at her. Another man is adjusting his tie looking in a mirror in the hall. He picks up his briefcase and walks past Katherine with a huge semen stain on his crotch. He must have blown his load at least twice for a stain that big. Katherine's eyes widen, and her mouth is agape by what she sees.

They enter Ernesto's office, where there is a large mahogany desk with a huge cabinet behind it. On the desk is a large cloth with something under it. He removes the cloth to reveal a disassembled pistol. The pistol was originally a gift from a client, and he goes out for target practice from time to time. One day he went out shooting, and the gun didn't fire. Convinced something inside the gun was blocking the bullet, he slowly and carefully took the gun apart. He cleaned each piece and is now trying to put it back together, but he can't remember which parts go where. So every day he tries to do a little reassembling. This is the eighth week he has been trying to put his gun back together.

Katherine sits in the seat across from him and watches him unshamelessly trying to put that gun together. She has a very disgusted look on her face.

Ernesto sees this look and assumes she's looking at the gun parts. "You don't know how to put a gun back together, do you?" he asks in a nonchalant way.

She sits up in the chair across from his desk and is seething at what she sees. "You run a whorehouse! I can't believe this is what you do!" she bellows.

Ernesto continues trying to put together the gun and doesn't even look up. "High-class call girls," he says, correcting her.

"You said you were a human-resources manager."

"They are human. They are resources, and I manage them."

"You're disgusting!" Katherine says as she sits up in her chair, using a tone that demands an explanation.

Ernesto finally looks up at her. He studies her face and expression for a while. He rolls his chair back and stands up. "Really?" he asks inquisitively. He slowly makes his way to his office door.

"This is how you make your money?" Katherine says with her voice rising as her anger also rises.

Ernesto opens the door and starts speaking his native language of Tagalog. A few minutes later, four young ladies walk into his office in a straight line.

Katherine is in awe at what she sees. All four are the most perfect examples of the epitome of beauty that you can imagine. Not a blemish or flaw on any inch of their skin. Their body tone is flawless, with not an ounce of unwanted fat. Their breasts should be bronzed because of their natural perkiness and shape. Their hair is of different colors and lengths, but all have hair that is shiny and full, with plenty of body. The women all look as if they should be advertising products for hair, teeth, and skin. That's how perfect they are!

Ernesto is amazed at the expression on Katherine's face and then says, "None of my girls have been altered in any way through surgical procedures. Several areas of this planet contain exceptionally beautiful people. One area is the Philippines. Unfortunately, because of the abject poverty there, some Filipino families can't care for their children, so they sell them people who can provide for them."

Katherine is at first appalled, but she has heard of these stories before from Eugenia. She can't believe how incredibly lovely these girls are. One girl in particular is more beautiful than the others. She also looks extremely young to be working there.

Ernesto notices her looking at Lailani. Ernesto says something else in Tagalog, and Lailani moves next to him. He puts his arm around her, much as a father would comfort a daughter.

Katherine is stunned. "How old is that girl?" she asks.

Ernesto moves closer to Katherine with his arm still firmly around Lailani. He looks her square in the eye and says, "I used the money you gave me to get her into this country. I had several high-end clients who couldn't wait to have sex with this sixteen-year-old girl. They were lining up to be with her. That's how I was able to double your money. Now, if you are so disgusted, you can just give back the extra five thousand." Ernesto takes his arm from around Lailani and extends his hand out to Katherine, hoping she will fill it with the money.

Katherine stands there for a few moments grappling with the dilemma. Considering her and Edwyn's present financial situation, there's no way Katherine can give this money back, no matter how it was earned. In fact, she never knew money could be doubled so quickly. However, the money was earned because several middle-aged men had sex with a clearly underage prostitute. Katherine justifies it this way: she did not know the initial five grand was to be used to bring this girl into the country. Her initial payment is due her, and that's a fact. The other five grand is almost like—no, it's exactly like—a dividend. She continues to stare at Ernesto's still outstretched hand. Still a little embarrassed to say anything, she just shakes her head no.

"I didn't think so," he says, knowing she would never have given back the money. He takes out a newspaper with the arrest of Bernie Madoff on the front page and shows it to Katherine.

"Did you see Bernie Madoff was arrested for that Ponzi scheme?" Ernesto asks.

"Yes, I did."

Then Ernesto asks, "Did you invest with him? Be honest."

"Yes, I did," Katherine answers, barely opening her mouth.

Ernesto now moves around her in a semicircle and then finally stands behind his desk like a lawyer presenting his closing argument to the judge. "If you knew how he made his money, would you have still invested with him?" Ernesto asks. Katherine stays silent because she knows the answer would most likely be yes. Ernesto continues. "Your husband got laid off, right?"

"He was bought out of his contract, actually."

"Whatever," Ernesto says, waving her off and continuing his argument. "He used to work for a brokerage firm? Where? Asset management, fixed income, mortgage-backed securities? Well, these girls are funds in my portfolio. The better they perform, the better the return on my investment. If one doesn't perform to expectations, she is replaced with another. Remember the old Smith Barney slogan? We make our money the old-fashioned way too. We fuck you so good, you'll give us your money with a smile on your face. So don't look down on me because of the way I make money."

Katherine starts laughing to herself and thinks everything he has said is true. There really isn't much difference between white-collar and blue-collar crime. One man can rob a bank and another man can rob people through a Ponzi scheme, and both can get the same amount of jail time. Who's the bigger criminal? Twenty years ago a white-collar criminal would have gotten five or maybe ten years in jail. That was considered a heavy sentence in those days. Now, some of them get as many years as mass murderers and terrorists. These kinds of people have always looked down on murderers and terrorists.

"Does Eugenia know about this?" Katherine asks.

Ernesto gives a sarcastic grin and says, "Of course she does. How do you think she *got* into this country?"

For a few minutes, Katherine has fleeting images of a much younger Eugenia performing fellatio on a middle-aged man who will probably achieve orgasm in forty-two seconds. She then thinks some more and realizes that after Eugenia reached a certain age and couldn't fuck for cash, she had no real skills left, leaving her no choice but to do domestic work. What a sad life indeed.

Ernesto continues. "Who I am, what I do, and the way I do it makes me part of a club. A club where you don't rat anybody out, and you always keep your mouth shut. An exclusive club where people realize early on you have to rob to get rich in this life. The line between how your husband used to make his money and how I make mine is so thin that if you closed your eyes, you couldn't tell the difference. So don't judge me. Otherwise, you can go fuck off back to your suburban utopia dreamland."

In the midst of his passionate speech lecturing Katherine on the moral fibers of our financial times, his thumb is slightly punctured by the spring from the gun, causing him to draw it back and put it in his mouth, shouting, "Fuck!"

As he tries to suck the pain and blood out of his thumb, Katherine comes around to his side of desk. "What are you trying to do?" she asks almost innocently.

Ernesto looks at her, almost annoyed, and says, "The gun won't fire, and I'm trying to put this fucking thing back together, and I can't."

Katherine looks at him the same way you would look at a mentally challenged person when you ask him or her something as simple as his or her name. She scans the table, making sure all of the necessary parts are there, and then she rather skillfully puts the gun back together. For extra measure, she cocks it and pulls the trigger a few times. "You need to put some lubricant on the cylinder pin and ratchet. It's a little stiff. That's probably why you thought it wasn't working properly."

Ernesto sits there, unable to say anything. He looks at this blond, blue-eyed woman, who shouldn't be able to know what a gun looks like, much less that this one needs lubricant. Added to that, she has been able to put it together with such ease, it makes him wonder who she really is. "How the fuck did you do that?" he asks.

Across Katherine's face appears the most satisfying smile she can create. "My husband belongs to a club too, a club where people like you couldn't consider becoming a member. We might have you park our cars, get our drinks and food, and wash our toilets. My father belonged to a club when I was younger, and they had a large firing range. My job was to take the guns apart and clean them. This club had a smaller range, and when there was a problem with any of the guns, they called me."

The last comment piques Ernesto's interest, and he asks her, "What other jobs did you have at the club?"

Katherine smiles slightly at this because she knows exactly what Ernesto is implying. Ernesto smiles as well. "I went there fishing, and I caught myself a husband," she says with sly pride.

Ernesto goes into his desk and pulls out a standard stun gun, which was another gift from a client of his. He hands it to Katherine, who takes it without a hint of reluctance. "Does it work?" she asks before pulling the trigger and watching the electricity flow between the two probes. "And there's my answer. How powerful is it?"

"It'll put a three-hundred-pound man on his ass," Ernesto tells her.

At this point, Amelia comes back into the room looking more nervous than the last time she spoke to Ernesto. "Sorry, Ernie," she says pensively, approaching him with caution.

"What now?" he says, adjusting himself and bracing for the bad news to come.

Amelia takes a deep breath and says, "Well, there are two things: client number eight is here."

Ernesto puts his hand up, letting her know he understands and is in charge. "Well, put him in room four and tell him to wait. Alexandra hasn't gotten here yet," he says without skipping a beat.

Amelia lets out a deep sigh and says, "That's the other thing. She was arrested last night and won't be coming in. They wanted to make a deal with her for a reduced sentence if she gave us up. She told them to fuck off, so she'll probably go to jail for about two years and then be deported. She says she'll see us about six months after that."

Ernesto lets out a hearty laugh at the thought of her sneaking back into the country that banished her. He looks directly at Katherine. "See? That's a wise investment. I'll get a great return on her." Ernesto swings his chair around and opens the large cabinet, which has monitors of every room in the house. Some are occupied with girls working, while others are empty. He scans to room four and sees client number eight sitting there taking his suit jacket and tie off. He goes to the control panel that operates the cameras to get a closer look at the man's face. Katherine sees this, and her mouth gapes open. She can hardly believe what she is seeing.

"He's a new client and has been coming in here pretty steadily every week for a few months. He pays up front, which is good. What the fuck am I going to do with him now?"

Katherine stands up and moves closer to the monitor to get a better look at his face, to see if the man is who she thinks it is. It is unmistakably who that is. She is sure of it. "I know that guy," Katherine says with self-assurance.

Ernesto turns to her curiously. "How do you know him?"

⋏

Katherine takes a deep breath and begins to relate the story of how she and George met. "I've been to many extravagant company parties, and usually they're held at huge hotels or on nighttime cruises. One time, they rented out an entire theater in the theater district, and we saw a private impromptu show complete with singing, tap dancing, and people swinging from the ceiling. But this was the first time they rented out a dance club. It was weird because usually people at the firm are pretty stuffy and don't go for that kind of venue.

"Edwyn and I pulled up to the club, which was called Arena. Quite honestly, it didn't look like much from the outside. I was amazed at how big it was: the dance floor, the eating areas, and the many corners to sit and socialize. After we checked our coats, we were just looking around at how big the place was when George and his wife, Elizabeth, came up to us. Elizabeth had been looking great recently. I knew she went to the gym and had a personal trainer to concentrate on her upper arms, abs, and ass. I guess she wanted to look good for her own self-esteem as well as for George. Not that it made a difference, since George would look at anything with two tits, a hole, and a heartbeat.

"We mingled for a bit with them until I had to excuse myself to the ladies room. I felt George's eyes on my ass as I walked away, and, to prove the point, I turned back fast enough to just to catch him looking away. The bathrooms weren't really labeled male or female because the attendants usually would let people know which was which. But since the party had just started, and only a few people were there, it wouldn't matter which bathroom I used. While in the stall taking a pee, I heard someone come in, and I thought nothing of it until the door opened and I saw George standing there with his hand on his zipper.

"'Wha…' I shouted, shocked that a man was standing there watching me piss.

"George was actually frozen in fear, not expecting to see me there. 'I'm sorry! I'm so sorry!' he shouted right away. Then a funny thing happened. The shock of him opening the door on someone peeing wore off, and he realized he'd opened the door on me! He stood there for a few seconds watching me take a piss until I slammed the door in his face so fast the wind totally messed up my hair.

"Then he panicked again. 'What the fuck was I thinking? Kat, I'm so sorry. I can't believe I just did that!'

"As I wiped myself, I could still hear George apologizing to me, and as I exited the stall, he was standing there in the middle of the room.

"'It's fine. It was an honest mistake,' I told him.

"'It's not like I saw anything,' he responded slyly.

"'Actually, you saw everything.' I paused slightly and lowered my voice. 'Everything.'

"I don't think I'd ever seen George turn that shade of white. He actually looked like he was about to have a stroke.

Well, since you saw me pee, it's only fair that I see you pee, too,' I said to him in almost a hushed tone.

"He stood there for a few seconds, thinking I was joking. I assured him I was not, and if he wanted to have a private moment with me, he needed to get to business before someone else came in. He slowly moved to a stall, and I stood on the toilet in the next stall and looked over the partition and marveled at how healthy George's penis looked. If there was a game show where you had to guess a man's age based on how his penis looked, I would be way off by about twenty-five years with George. I knew he worked out a lot, but wow!

"Anyway, I decided to have a little fun with him and whispered how thick and manly his member was and how I was surprised his wife could walk erect with that thing in his pants and what a handful he must be. He started laughing like a little boy, and he started to get hard—so hard, in fact, that when he started peeing, the flow of urine went completely over the toilet and he was peeing on the floor! I asked him where the fire was, and he started laughing again. When I started making fire engine siren noises, he totally lost it, and there was pee in the toilet, on the toilet, on the seat, and on the floor. I started to leave and thanked him for a wonderful time, and he showed a lot of concern, wondering what to do with his now-erect penis.

I looked at him with the bulge in his pants and asked how long he would be like that.

"'I don't know! I hope just a few minutes.'

"I moved closer to him, smiled, and said, 'Well, in that case…' I took it out and started stroking his cock almost violently, to the point where he might explode. I had this devilish grin on my face, watching his eyes rolling to the back of his head as he breathed heavily.

"The attendant came in, and George turned around to put his horse back in the stable. I then walked out of the bathroom, leaving him with a rock-hard dick at a company party with his wife and all of his coworkers. For the rest of the evening, everywhere I was, George was close by. I went onto the dance floor, and he grabbed the first woman close to him and danced right next to me. I sat down to eat a little bit, and he sat right next to me. It got to the point where everyone noticed he was following around me like a goat in heat. His wife even pulled him to the side to ask why he was following me. He of course denied it, saying it was a party and you're going to run into people, blah, blah, blah. But we all knew. At least I knew."

⋏

When Katherine finishes the story, she starts to think back to that night and remembers how George followed her around. She then starts to think about how good she looked in that dress and how she had to sell it because money was getting tight. She starts to think about the lifestyle she used to have and the life she has now and wonders how things can change so fast. She is so lost in thought, she doesn't notice Ernesto looking at her with a devilish smile. She comes to her senses and looks at him very warily. "What?" she says.

Ernesto gets up from his desk and sits in the chair next to Katherine. "When was the last time you saw him?"

"Not sure. It's been a while."

Ernesto moves a little closer and asks, "Does he still have the hots for you?"

"I'm almost positive. Why do you ask?" Katherine says, moving back from him.

Ernesto doesn't answer her, but then, he doesn't have to. The way he's looking Katherine up and down lets her know he wants her to go in that room where George is. When she realizes this, Katherine jumps up, shocked. "You don't expect me to..." She finds the whole situation so repulsive and difficult, she can't even finish what she is saying.

Ernesto stands up slowly and walks toward her, the way an adult would a child when trying to give that child advice on how to break the law. "These girls are not hookers on Hunter's Point getting five dollars for a blow job. These are professionals who charge a few thousand dollars for their services. Someone who looks like you, on a guy like that, can charge more."

Katherine paces the floor, looking down when she has a moment of clarity. She stops walking, looks up, turns around to Ernesto, and says, "How much more?" Ernesto smiles wide as Katherine looks at the cabinet with the monitors and says, "Can you videotape what's going on in that room?"

Ernesto goes back to his desk, sits in his chair, and swings it around to face the console. "Yup. We use it as insurance against people who don't pay or who are assholes."

Katherine moves closer to the screen. "You mean like that guy from earlier?" she asks.

"Exactly," he says. "Why do you ask?"

"Tape the room we're in," Katherine says with decisiveness. She lets out a sly grin.

⅄

She enters the room wearing the same clothes she had on this morning, which are nothing special.

George is sitting on the bed, but when he sees Katherine, he jumps up, shocked and dismayed. "Oh!" he exclaims. "I was just about to go out there and see what the problem is."

Katherine, who is still slowly walking in George's direction, says, "The other girl couldn't make it, so when I told Ernesto about how you followed me around during the Christmas party that year, he asked me to come off the bench to lend some *ass*istance," she says while putting a hand on his leg.

He looks at her hand and laughs nervously, saying, "You still remember that?"

Katherine moves a little closer to him and says, "Everybody remembers that." Even though she hasn't really done more than touch his leg, she can already see his nature rise. "Someone's happy to see me," Katherine says as she moves sleekly and seductively toward George. She sits very close to him and crosses her legs in such a way that they drape over his.

George ogles her body, but this time with shame. He stares at her natural blond shoulder-length hair, which flows with the sensuality of sirens in Greek mythology. Her lips, fingers, and toes, all painted red and against her skin, make for an alluring contrast. Also of note, she has what can only be called the perfect set of breasts. They are not too large or too small. In fact, they are an almost perfect circle of sexual satisfaction, with nipples like little soldiers standing at attention to salute your lips. At her age and level of exercise, it would be many years before her tits would know the meaning of the word "breast ptosis."

"You move like a cat. I like cats," George says with pride now that his penis is so hard he can probably cut diamonds.

Slowly unbuttoning his shirt, she says, "And this is where you go, 'I hear the firm is doing pretty well.'"

George, clearly more interested in getting naked than answering questions, tries to help her undress, but she slaps his hand away.

This temporarily snaps him back to answer the question. "Yeah. Better than I expected. Work has picked up quite a bit." George leans back on the bed and lets her undress him. She finger walks across his legs to his now-throbbing penis.

"You know, Edwyn left you a message. You think there's any way for you to get him his old job back?" she asks as she makes finger swirls on his testicles.

George temporarily loses it by laughing out loud like a little boy. He regains his composure long enough to say, "I don't know. I may need some convincing."

Katherine unbuckles his pants and moves his undergarments aside to reveal his still-impressive member. She grabs it firmly and shakes it for toughness, as you would a piece of meat you are thinking about buying at a butcher store. She then looks at George and says, "Let me help you think." And without another word, she performs fellatio on George by moving her head back and forth, up and down, and in semicircular motions.

The reality of this moment is almost too much for George. His face displays such expressions of ecstasy that, to the untrained eye, it might look as if he's having a seizure. Katherine now uses one hand to aid in his release and the other to cradle his testicles.

Back in Ernesto's office, he has called some of the girls in to watch this impressive performance. Some of them are taking notes. Ernesto stands up closer to the screen and says, "You see how she's moving her head like that? That's what you need to do. That's how Americans like to get their dicks sucked."

Some girls nod and jot that down.

"Her head moves so fast! Look at that!" one girl says. Off in the corner, a girl fairly new to the trade asks almost innocently, "You think she's done this before?" All of the girls now look at Ernesto, very curious about the answer.

He looks at all of them, goes to his chair, leans back, smiles, and says, "I suspect there's a lot of things she's done before."

And one at a time, all of them look back to the screen as Katherine makes George climax so strongly that he nearly passes out. The sounds he makes while doing so can only be described as a howler monkey who has finally gotten the engine started on his 1977 Chevy Nova.

Amelia then turns to Ernesto and says, "This is kind of perverted. Should we even be watching this?"

Ernesto doesn't even turn in Amelia's direction. "Membership has its privileges," Ernesto says, almost as a throwaway line. They are all still amazed George is still going for a man his age.

CHAPTER 4

Unlike the vast pseudo-opulence of the Collingsworth home, the Kinney home is much more subdued. While the Collingsworths like for people to appreciate their wealth by viewing their paintings, chandeliers, and other decadent furnishings, the Kinneys have taken the opposite approach. Their home is actually worth more than the Collingsworth home, so Arlene and Brett have decided to let the beauty of the home speak for itself. They have a huge foyer that leads to a large curved staircase made of solid mahogany. The kitchen has all the latest and greatest appliances, the curtains were all handmade, and the beds have the finest linens.

Brett and Edwyn are sitting in Brett's sumptuous living room with drinks in their hands when Jabari comes in, breathing quite heavily and carrying a box of computer equipment. Brett sees this and immediately stands up, feeling bad for him. Edwyn cannot be bothered. "Where does this go?" Jabari says through breaths.

"Are you crazy? Do you know how heavy that box is?" Brett says with concern. He tries to take the box away, but Jabari pulls it back, letting him know he can handle it. Jabari is quite strong even though he doesn't look it.

"I thought you were going to help me," Jabari says to Edwyn, who still hasn't had a reason to get out of his chair.

"You're doing great!" Edwyn says as he sips more brandy.

Brett, still feeling bad, puts his hand on Jabari's shoulder. "Upstairs, last door on the left," he says and doesn't sit back down until Jabari is out of sight as he huffs and puffs up the stairs. Brett sits back down and meets eyes with Edwyn, who doesn't seem to have a care. Brett again looks up at the stairs and is about to ask why he didn't help since that was the reason they both came over to the house in the first place.

"You were saying about your father-in-law's will," Edwyn says, wanting to get back to the point after being so rudely interrupted by Jabari.

"Uhh, we're meeting with the lawyers tomorrow to discuss all of the old man's holdings," Brett says, not that interested.

Edwyn is very curious about what the old man had in his portfolio and, more importantly, what Brett stands to gain in the inheritance. Edwyn asks, "Did he have gold?"

Brett shoots him a side-eye glance. "Not sure about that, but I know he had cattle. About four hundred head. Arlene just told me," Brett says, nonchalant, looking away, almost as if he's thinking of something else.

Meanwhile, Edwyn has actually put his drink down and is now very attentive. He wants to know, or at least have an idea, how much they'll get. He asks the question straightforwardly because of their relationship.

Brett hesitates at first but then relents and tells Edwyn. He was, after all, Brett's mentor. "Millions," Brett mumbles.

Edwyn's eyes grow very wide imagining that word: millions. How much? Tens of millions? Edwyn starts thinking about that amount of money to the point where he is actually becoming erect. Brett, though, doesn't seem impressed by that at all. Edwyn sees this and wonders why he doesn't seem interested, but, deep down, Edwyn knows why.

"You say that amount like it's no big deal," Edwyn says, wishing he were in that position.

Brett looks up at the ceiling toward the floor above him where his wife is and says, "Money isn't everything."

⅄

Jabari drops off the box in the assigned bedroom and starts to leave. On his way downstairs, he spots Arlene in a newly finished nursery. All of the walls are painted blue, with huge clouds all around and a happy-faced sun on the ceiling right above the crib, and, in the crib itself, are toys and a hanging mobile that will give more than enough stimulation. The room is complete, with one exception: no baby. Without a baby, the room will never be complete. Arlene isn't concerned with the amount of money she will inherit from her late wayward father—or anything else, for that matter. She's still going to the specialist and still holding out hope.

Arlene is so lost in thought she doesn't even hear Jabari walk in behind her. He looks around and the room and marvels at the paint job.

"Nice sun," he comments while looking at the ceiling.

Arlene nearly jumps out of her skin, causing Jabari to jump as well. Neither one wanted to startle the other.

Jabari puts his hand on her shoulder and says, "I didn't mean to scare you. I was just commenting on how pretty the room looks. You did this by yourself? It looks like it was professionally done."

Arlene looks up at the ceiling with beaming pride and says, "I did. Every drop of paint in this room was done by my hand."

They both continue to look around the room. Jabari tries not to ask about them having a baby. He knows they are having a hard time trying to have a baby but is not sure why. He will never ask because it is a very sensitive subject.

"When did you get here?" Arlene asks, knowing how awkward the situation is getting.

"Just a few minutes ago. We were helping Brett with some computer equipment, but the 'we' is turning into just 'me.'"

Arlene is almost afraid to ask but is required to at this point. "We?" she asks.

Jabari tenses up as he delivers his answer. "Edwyn and I came together," he says sheepishly.

And with that, Arlene takes a deep sigh as her body falls and her back curves just a little. The light that was in her eyes in her room of solace has now been extinguished. It's as if the mere mention of Edwyn's name has put her in a physical state of depression. Jabari knows Arlene has never cared for Edwyn, but this is the first time Jabari has ever seen that kind of transformation. He briefly tries to fathom what Edwyn could have done, but knowing Edwyn, it could have been anything. Jabari starts to slowly back out of the room. "I should get going," he says.

Arlene follows him, saying, "I'll walk you out."

Back downstairs, Edwyn is still plying Brett for information on his financial windfall, while Brett's concern is for his wife who has just lost her father. "I wish I could do something for her," Brett says, very concerned.

Edwyn is much more enthusiastic with his response. "Are you kidding? With all the money you'll inherit, you can take her to the best spas in the world. She'll be back to normal in no time!" Edwyn says, patting him on the back.

Brett forces a smile but drops it when Arlene and Jabari come down the stairs.

"Everything is set down, so if you don't need me, I'll shove off," Jabari says to Brett.

Brett's first priority is for his wife, who looks distressed again. "Where were you, honey?" he asks, very concerned.

"I was in the nursery when Jabari came in to admire my handiwork." She and Jabari look at each other and smile slightly.

"You guys still trying to have a baby?" Edwyn says with a slight smile on his face, careful to not make eye contact with Arlene, who rolls her eyes at him in such a way that everybody notices it.

"Yes. We are. We're not giving up," Brett says.

Jabari looks at Brett and Arlene and says, "Good for you. I know it's been hard, losing your father."

Arlene then looks at Jabari, cuts her eyes at Edwyn again, and has a slightly evil thought. Edwyn has made her uncomfortable, so she should return the favor.

"Oh, Jabari, you know what that's like. Your father died some time ago in some kind of accident, right?"

Jabari looks at Arlene and realizes she is trying to make Edwyn so uncomfortable that he will leave. Jabari is very sensitive about the death of his

father. He glances over to Edwyn and then back to Arlene, who is still looking at Edwyn.

Now it's Jabari's turn for his body to fall a little. "Some say accident; others say murder."

At this point, Edwyn would love to be anywhere other than his current
location. He starts to move toward the front door. "We should really be going," Edwyn says almost frantically.

Arlene cuts her eyes at Edwyn again and with a smile says, "So soon?"

Brett tries to diffuse the situation by putting one hand on Jabari's shoulder and extending the other one. Jabari gives Brett a long, warm, and genuine
handshake. Edwyn can only look on jealously. "Thanks for your help, Jabari.
If you ever need anything, don't hesitate to call me," Brett says with a kind
smile.

Jabari gives a knowing nod and moves toward the door as Edwyn holds
it open for him. He finally catches Arlene's eye.

"See you around, Eddie," Arlene says.

"You know I don't like people calling me that," Edwyn says, more serious now.

"Yeah. I know, Eddie," she responds, not giving a fuck what Edwyn
thinks.

Edwyn tries to smile, but even he's not convinced as they leave.

Λ

In the car on their way home, Jabari is driving, and Edwyn is riding shotgun. Both men are lost in thought, though for very different reasons. Jabari
is really starting to wonder why Arlene doesn't like Edwyn. They've always
had a cold and distant relationship, but for the last few years, the animosity
between the two has been ramped up, particularly with Arlene. "Why does
Arlene hate you so much?" Jabari says finally, as his curiosity has gotten the
best of him.

Edwyn stares straight ahead, not saying anything.

Jabari is starting to ask again when Edwyn finally says, "They have a nice
house, right?"

The question stops Jabari's train of thought. He has no idea where that question came from. He pauses for a moment. "Sure, it's beautiful," he says hesitantly.

Edwyn turns down the radio, which was already on very low volume. He wants to make sure he has Jabari's complete attention.

Edwyn adjusts himself in the seat and says, "You know how many times I've been to that house? I know all the ins and outs of the house. For example, I know that for years, they have never locked their back door."

Jabari is actually surprised by this. In fact, neither he nor his wife can go to sleep without locking all the windows and doors.

"Really? They don't? Why not?"

Edwyn smiles a little now because he wants Jabari to be roped in by that question. Now that he has Jabari's full attention, he is going to let Jabari know why he is being told all this.

"Are you kidding? They live in a very expensive home with an alarm they never use because they feel the neighborhood is so safe. Why bother taking extra precautions? I helped him pick out almost every piece of furniture, including the safe, which I know the combination of."

Jabari pulls the car over and turns off the engine. He turns in Edwyn's direction and looks him square in the eye. "Why are you telling me this?"

Edwyn then turns to Jabari and says, "Because you're going to rob him for me."

Jabari just stares at him in utter disbelief because he has known Edwyn for a long time and knows when he's serious.

⁁

At his house, Jabari walks in, still so stunned by what Edwyn said that he doesn't notice that his wife, Sabriah, has rearranged the furniture again. Ever since they moved to their current apartment three years ago, she has been watching home-decor shows religiously to get new ideas on how to position their furniture. Considering she is only five foot five and about 110 pounds, the fact she was able to move a couch; two chairs, one leather and one fabric; a coffee table; two lamps; and a wall unit is quite impressive.

Now she stands with her back to him as she uses a wall to stretch her back. She turns around to see him and doesn't notice his mood or face. She stands back so he can get a better look at what she's done today. "What do you think? I figured if we move the couch to this side, there would be more room in the middle. Good idea? I know you think I watch the home-decor channel too much, right?" Sabriah finally notices his face and moves toward him. She drops her smile and gets dead serious. "What happened?"

Jabari slowly looks at her and sighs deeply.

CHAPTER 5

George took a great sense pride when he got Edwyn's old office. He was always envious that his office was much smaller than Edwyn's. That was one of the reasons why George was so involved in Edwyn's firing from the firm. When George finally got a chance to move to the new space, he didn't change a thing. A corner office with a large mahogany desk with a matching bookcase and a view that is, in a word, breathtaking. From his office on the seventy-eighth floor, he can see all of Manhattan, part of Jersey, and Staten Island. A fully stocked bar near the sitting room with large leather chairs. He has a loyal secretary named Debra, who protects his interests from everybody, including his wife; what George says goes, and he can stay in his private bathroom as long as he wants. No wonder he stays in his office more than he does at home.

Debra walks in with a legal-sized envelope and hands it to him.

George looks at it, very confused. "What's this?" he asks.

Debra walks to the doorway, turns, and says, "Not sure. A messenger just dropped it off five minutes ago. And your wife is on the phone."

She goes back to her desk as George picks up the phone. "Hey, honey. Getting in some shopping?"

Elizabeth has always worked very hard on her marriage by buying sexy lingerie, trying different perfumes, and staying in shape. She's at the Westchester, a high-end shopping mall in White Plains, New York, trying on some fancy and sexy clothes. She realized early on that to keep a marriage healthy, one has to never stop trying to surprise. Elizabeth has always been way too trusting. naive that way.

"Yes! I found those earrings we saw before," she says, very cheerful.

As they talk, George opens the envelope and pulls out a letter that reads, "Are you sure there's no way?" George is very confused by this.

"Very good, honey. What's up? I'm kind of busy here," George says to his wife without trying to sound very confused by the note.

"Not much. I was just wondering what that note meant," Elizabeth says.

"What note?" George says, even more confused.

"There was a note outside the door after you left. It said, 'Are you sure there's no way?' What does that mean?" Elizabeth asks.

Suddenly his face turns white, and his heart to starts pound rapidly. He takes out the rest of the contents of the envelope and sees pictures of him and Katherine in various stages of undress and in sexual positions. Some of the pictures are quite graphic, and all of them are embarrassing. He stares at the pictures so long that he doesn't hear Elizabeth's question. "Sorry; say that again?" he says, very much at a loss for words.

"You're not even listening to me. I said, 'Did you send this letter?'" Elizabeth says with her voice rising slightly.

Clearly Katherine sent the pictures, but George is curious why she hasn't contacted him yet. He has to try to stall for time while he figures out the best way to deal with this situation.

"Where was it?" George asks in a bob-and-weave fashion.

"I told you. It was on the front door outside this morning," Elizabeth says, clearly getting more annoyed.

"What time?" George says again, with a voice that sounds as if he might be trying to find a handle on how to deal with Elizabeth until he can reach Katherine but isn't quite there. He knows he's upsetting his wife, but he just needs time to think.

"I'm not sure. Like I told you, when I left the house—"

"Liz? I thought that was you. How are you?" Katherine says with a huge smile.

"Kat! Hi!"

George listens to them hug, kiss, and make small talk, knowing full well that Katherine was probably following Elizabeth in the mall and waiting for the moment when Liz brought up the note to show herself. If Katherine tells Elizabeth about the pictures, George will be fucked in more ways than one.

"George, you'll never guess who it is. Remember Kat? Katherine Collingsworth?" Elizabeth says with genuine enthusiasm. Of course he remembers! After lusting after her for years, he finally had sex with her not a week ago. But he damn sure can't tell his wife that.

"Katherine..." he says, pretending to try to recall that name.

Elizabeth sucks her teeth and says, "Oh, you remember. You were hitting on her all night that one time at the company holiday party."

"Oh, you remember that," George says, laughing nervously.

"Everybody remembers that, George," Elizabeth says.

Katherine then makes her move toward Elizabeth. "Is that George? I would love to say hello."

George's first instinct is to yell no into the phone, but of course he can't do that, nor can he give anything away. He gets very nervous as he hears the phone being passed. He has to figure out what to say and how to say it to Katherine with his wife within an earshot.

Katherine grabs the phone and is extra upbeat when she says, "George? How are you?"

George immediately understands what she is doing and has to let her have her fun.

"Katherine," George responds, very monotone.

She ups the ante by saying, "It's been so long since I saw you last. You probably don't remember what I look like."

Elizabeth finds that line too tempting not to respond to, considering the Christmas party incident. She leans in to Katherine and says, "I doubt it. You were a knockout then and a knockout now. In fact, you look better now."

Katherine giggles like a little schoolgirl, seductively flips her hair, and says, "Why thank you, Liz."

At this point George is more angry than nervous and wants to know what exactly Katherine is up to. He covers the phone so no one in his office can hear him and through his teeth says, "What are you doing?"

Katherine smiles very devilishly. She has him right where she wants him. She's amazed at how easily George is being played.

"Edwyn's fine, George. He's just fine. Thanks for asking. Well, I won't keep you. Nice talking to you, George. Hope to speak again soon," she says with a slight playfulness.

Katherine then hands the phone back to Elizabeth, and George starts to loosen his grip on the phone as he hears their final exchange before Katherine walks away.

"Listen, I really have to go, but we must get together soon," Katherine says.

"Are you available for a quick bite now?" Liz says eagerly.

"I can't. I have to make an important phone call," Katherine says with a wink in her smile.

They kiss and hug again, and, as Katherine starts to back away from her, she takes out her cell phone. "I'm sure we'll see each other again," Katherine says to her before turning around and walking more swiftly while dialing her phone.

"It's so odd running into her after all these years," Elizabeth says. "What are the chances? She looks great! I mean, she really looks good. I'd fuck her. And if I would, I know you would. But don't get any ideas."

She's not one to curse, so she's more surprised at her own profanity. George fake laughs enough to get by and says, "How would I? I haven't seen her in years."

Elizabeth grunts in agreement and then says, "What were we talking about before I ran into Kat? Oh yeah, the note. What did you mean by that?"

Fuck! George was hoping she would forget the whole thing until tonight. At least he would have more time to come up with something. George has no more time for stalling. Here goes the Hail Mary. "What? Wait, remember when I wanted to go on that Italian cruise, and you said it might be too expensive?" George says as he winces with one eye closed to see if the lie would fly.

At this point, Debra walks into his office and says, "Excuse me, but there's a Katherine Collingsworth on the phone for you."

"Can you shut the door, please?" George figured she would be calling. "Honey, I have to take this call, but we'll talk tonight, OK?" he says as Debra quietly shuts the door.

"Italian cruise? I don't remember us talking about an Italian cruise," Elizabeth says, almost not listening to anything George has said.

He's a little more impatient with his wife. "Did you hear me? I have to take this call. We'll talk tonight," George finally says before switching her off and picking up Katherine. Now that his wife is not listening, he can finally let Katherine have it. "Kat?" he says with much annoyance.

Katherine is much more upbeat when she says, "Nice talking to you again."

At this point, George totally loses it. "What the fuck are you doing?" he says. His blood boils and his pressure rises as he seethes in anger.

Katherine remains calm, almost stoic, until she finally says, "My problem is I don't know what's worse: telling your firm you're embezzling funds for high-priced call girls or telling your wife you've been embezzling funds from your firm to pay for high-priced call girls."

There is silence for a few seconds, and George lets this all sink in. Katherine is still very calm on her end, waiting for George to react. Finally George says, "What do you want?"

Katherine decides to pour it on a little. She takes out her copy of the pictures. "You like those pictures I sent you? They were many, but I only gave you my favorites. I had those blown up because I know how you like to be blown up."

He looks at the pictures again, but this time he is seeing them through the eyes of his wife or employer or police or the media. It's so easy to get things onto the Internet these days and almost impossible to take them down. Maybe the pictures are already on the web and George just doesn't know it yet. No. Kat wouldn't do that. At least, not until she gets what she wants. "What the fuck do you want?" George demands again.

There is another pause, Katherine purposely making him wait. "You are going to get Edwyn his old job back at the firm," she says defiantly. She tells him as if it's a command or an order in the military where the other person doesn't really have a choice in the matter.

George thinks of the parameters of the situation and finds no solution. "Look, Kat, there's nothing I can do. It's out of my hands. That's a company decision that would have to come from up top. You have to understand that. I wish there were something I personally could do, but I don't have the authority to make that kind of decision, OK?" he says this with passion and commitment. Although the statement isn't entirely true, there is no need to let Katherine know that. Again, his main goal is to stall for time while he thinks of solutions.

Katherine is undeterred. She takes a deep breath and then says, "We usually have dinner at seven thirty. The first thing you are going to do is to call him at that time exactly. You will make up some excuse for not calling him sooner. You will be upbeat when talking to him. You will engage him. You will laugh at his corny jokes. And if he asks to get together for drinks, dinner, or anything, you will say very enthusiastically, 'I'd love to!' Do you understand me?"

George, now defeated, complies with her demands. "Why are you doing this?" he asks. Not that it matters, though.

There is a long pause on the phone until Katherine clears her throat and says, "You know what my father used to do? He was a salesman. You know what he sold? Shoes. Men's and women's shoes, and he was good at it. He was able to look at anybody, figure them out, and sell the kind of shoes they needed to make them look better. My father always said, it's not what you do, but how good you look doing it. People never care what's on the inside, just the outside. They only care about appearances. That's why people spend so much money on clothes, shoes, gym memberships, personal trainers, and, when all else fails, plastic surgery. He told me to always take care of the outside, and the inside will take care of itself.

"I wasn't so sure about the inside taking care of itself, but as far as the outside was concerned, I knew what to do and how do to it. I always took care of my body. Every single solitary inch of my body is absolute perfection: my ass, my legs, my tits, and my mouth. My father made sure I was exposed to the right things. I always had the right kind of friends who drove the right kinds of cars. I got into the right college, got into the right sorority, and, of course, sucked the right dicks. I always made sure I consorted with men who had excellent PP, or penis potential.

"You would never be caught having relations with someone who had neither the tools nor the talent to financially provide for you in the unforeseeable future in an unforeseeable economy. So talented was I in picking out the right mates, in college my moniker was the Cock Whisperer. And many men wanted me—including you, if you remember.

"I had my pick of the litter, but I chose Edwyn with cocksureness because he was right and had the most potential to provide me with the kind of life I always wanted. I'm not about to let a down economy and higher taxes interfere with my financial security. I want what every girl wants—to live in a mansion and be taken care of. Edwyn still has that potential, but he needs a little help. And that's where you and I come in. You are in the right position to help us, and you are going to help us because, quite frankly, I didn't sign on to be a trophy wife to end up in the poor house!" Katherine says before hanging up the phone.

George slowly puts the phone down and wonders what truly he has gotten himself into.

As Katherine walks away, she remembers the story of her sorority sister Aleta. She was like Katherine in that she had a beautiful body and had the attention of all of the guys and quite a few girls. Her main problem was her promiscuity. A man didn't have to do much to get into her pants. Katherine always said she would wind up with a man who talked a good game but was a loser. That man was Herbert. He was a music major, with jazz being his forte. There was also a rumor that he had the biggest natural cock on the East Coast. His nickname on campus was—you guessed it—Herbie Horsecock. They got together, got married, had kids, and he was a struggling musician for the rest of his life. She got tired of it, divorced him, and is now living back with her parents.

CHAPTER 6

Jabari arrives at the club for his shift. He parks his Toyota Echo in the employee parking area and walks inside. Employees are already there arranging the tables, polishing the furniture, and washing the floor.

He decides this time to walk through the kitchen to go to his locker. He rarely takes the kitchen route because, technically, he's not supposed to. Jabari has been in a daze ever since Edwyn proposed committing a crime to him. In fact, he is in such a fog, he doesn't even notice head Chef Michael drop a duck on the floor intended for his famous duck a l'orange. Jabari merely steps over the bird and continues walking. Chef Michael sees no need to throw away a perfectly cooked duck, so he places it back on the plate and continues as if nothing has happened, as do the other workers in the kitchen.

Jabari makes his way to his locker and stops short because of what greets him: a toy monkey hanging outside his locker door. He's always had it tough being the only black employee. Most of the members have been pretty nice to him, especially since his father died, but that has not excluded him from hearing certain comments from members under their breath in the past regarding the color of his skin. The worst one was probably Old Man Foster, who, when Jabari submitted to his request of shining his shoes but did a subpar job of it, said, "Back in my day, you people were the best shoe shiners in the world. Now look at you. Act like you're too good for that kind of work anymore. As far as I'm concerned, that's all you're good for."

Two weeks later, right when he was about to verbally abuse Jabari again, Old Man Foster had a massive heart attack right in front of him. He likes to think the last thing Old Man Foster saw before he died was the slight smile on Jabari's face.

He hadn't noticed anything overtly racist for about two weeks, since someone wrote "tar baby" on his locker. After this incident, and when Leonard tried to trip him earlier, he decided to prepare himself by taking photos of interesting things he had seen in and around the club—such as two weeks ago when chicken parts fell on the floor and were ultimately served, for example. Jabari wanted proof of these unsanitary conditions in case he needed it for legal purposes.

Now, as he takes his camera out and shoots several pictures of the monkey, Leonard and Harvey come over. They are like the nondynamic duo, with Leonard as Batman and Harvey as Robin. Harvey is a weak person who follows the crowd and does whatever Leonard says, and most times does so without thinking. There was also the rumor that they were secret lovers, but there was no proof.

"You don't have to take pictures of that. We was just fooling around," Leonard says in an intimidating way and reaches for the camera. Jabari stands his ground and stops him. Leonard then tries another tactic, attempting to riffle through his knapsack. "What's in here?" Leonard asks.

Jabari grabs him by the collar and slams him up against the lockers with such force that the door actually cracks open. Both Leonard and Harvey are surprised at how strong he is. Jabari then leans in close to Leonard and says, "Don't do that."

Leonard, who is almost off the ground, still tries to sound tough. "W-What are you going to do about it?" he says almost defiantly.

Jabari loosens his grip for a second, glances at Harvey and then back at Leonard, and says with a slight smile, "I'll tell everyone I caught you two slapping passed-out members in the head with your penises."

"They won't believe you," Leonard says.

Jabari smiles slightly and says, "They will when they see the pictures." Jabari doesn't really have pictures, but he wants to see if they'll take the bait.

Judging by the horrified look on Harvey's face, he would be too scared to call Jabari's bluff. Harvey leans close to Leonard and, almost in a whisper, says, "You told me no one would know." Leonard is shocked by Harvey's admission, embarrassed that Jabari has verbal confirmation and afraid the whole club will soon discover the truth. Knowing that Jabari has the upper hand, Leonard cowers, hoping that if Jabari feels he has the upper hand, he won't tell anyone and that he will release him. Sure enough, after a few minutes, Jabari lets him go.

Once Leonard adjusts himself, he says, "We just came in here to tell you that Edwyn wants to see you in his office."

Jabari puts his bag in his locker and walks past Harvey, who moves clear out of the way.

⋏

Jabari walks into Edwyn's office and sees that he is alone. He has always had mixed emotions whenever he's in there. He mostly wonders how many times his father was in there being forced to do things he would rather not. Edwyn's office is basically a monument to Edwyn. It has all of his accomplishments, from a club's point of view. All over the walls and his desk are trophies from his golfing rounds, tennis matches, and polo games, and the donations he has made to the local police department, hospital, and the urban youth center, although there was speculation he was forced to do that one. There are also plenty of pictures of prominent people in their time as well: judges, mayors, congressmen, and even a shot of Edwyn with the governor. Also, there are pictures of old staff who worked there and either retired or died.

One staff shot that catches Jabari's eye is the one with his father. Jabari takes the picture off the wall and stares at his father's face, forever frozen in time. How young and strong he was. Jabari has always wondered what his father was thinking in this shot because his facial expression is pretty stoic. He then notices a staff photo that he himself appears in. Oddly enough, he and his father are both standing in the same spot in both pictures. Also odd is that he has the same facial expression as his father. As Jabari looks at himself, he's trying to remember what he was thinking about in that shot. After a few minutes, it comes to him. He was thinking how this picture was going to stand for all time, and when he looked back thirty years from then, he would feel more embarrassment than nostalgia. Jabari is now thinking that his father was thinking the same thing. He holds both pictures up close to the light to see the similarities in their faces.

He is looking so intently that he doesn't notice Edwyn come in behind him. "Nice shots, huh?"

Jabari jumps when he hears Edwyn's voice. He turns to see Edwyn standing there with a glass of scotch in his hand. He puts his drink down, take both photos from Jabari, and puts them back in their respective places.

"You wanted to see me?" Jabari says in a businesslike monotone.

Edwyn picks up his drink and starts to walk out to the balcony. "Walk with me," he says.

It is quite cold outside, cold enough to see your breath. The cold, combined with the outdoor lights, casts long shadows on the floor. Considering the content of the conversation these two men are about to have, the mood seems very appropriate. Edwyn lights up a cigar and is quite calm, while Jabari is unusually nervous, given his normal calm demeanor.

"You want me to break into Brett and Arlene's house to steal?" Jabari asks, trying to confirm if Edwyn was serious or if Jabari heard him wrong.

"You know the kind of favors your father did for me, right?" Edwyn asks.

Jabari then tenses up and says, "I know one of those favors got him killed," almost as a reminder of their history.

Edwyn realizes he should not have started the conversation off like that, so he tries to smooth things over. "Your father's death was a tragic accident, and I mourn his loss every day." Jabari is unmoved by Edwyn's statement. "Your father was very close to suing me. He wanted to go after the club too, something about members being racist to him. He even hired that tough Jew lawyer, remember?"

Jabari stares into space, drawing a blank, and then finally says, "I don't remember that."

Edwyn chuckles a little and says, "Are you kidding? One of the old members fucked his father over years ago, and he's had a hard-on for us ever since. You don't even remember his name?"

Jabari looks at him with steely eyes and says, "That was a very low point in my life, and I don't remember much. But I do remember what you promised my father." He gives a knowing look to Edwyn, who acknowledges it by turning away.

Edwyn takes a deep breath and says, "I had to promise him not to involve you in any illegal activity." And with that line, Jabari gives Edwyn a look that says this entire conversation is a complete contradiction to what he promised. Edwyn is on the ropes and he knows it, but he is confident enough to think he can still persuade Jabari to help him. Jabari stands directly under one of the lights, and Edwyn follows and stands right next to him. "But these are hard economic times. Who could have predicted this?" Edwyn says.

"But I thought you and Brett were friends. You were his mentor, for goodness' sake. I mean, I know his wife hates you, but that's no reason to do this," Jabari says.

Edwyn takes a step back and ponders what Jabari just said, rolling his eyes. "Hates me. She should thank me for what I did for both of them."

"Did what?" Jabari asks. He always had a theory as to why Arlene never liked Edwyn. He is now going to see if that theory is correct.

Edwyn takes a deep breath and then says, "Brett was one of the best and brightest, top of his class. I met with Brett, and it went very well until Arlene spilled a drink all over my brand-new custom-made shirt. Damn thing cost me three hundred fifty dollars. That was the first time I wore it, and I never wore it again. He and Arlene were dating for a while, and it was pretty serious. They were going to plan a life together. This job would have been the platform for them to do just that. But after she spilled the drink, his stock went way down, and she knew it. Arlene did not want to be the reason why Brett wouldn't get the job. She didn't want to jeopardize this opportunity."

Jabari looks at him, very intrigued. "So?"

"So…"

⋏

Edwyn takes a deep breath and tells Jabari what happened next.

"In the hotel bathroom, I was standing there with my shirt off, trying desperately to get the stain out with club soda. The frustration was all over my face as I was scrubbing away. There was a knock at the door, which I assumed was the porter who had made the club soda recommendation in the first place. As the knocking got more frequent and louder, I slammed the shirt down in the sink filled with running water. I marched over to the door barking, 'This fucking club soda isn't working! You told me it would. You know what? I want my money back.' I swung the door open, only to find Arlene standing there. I poked my head out to see if the porter was with her. She was alone. 'Arlene?' I said, very confused and slightly annoyed.

"'Hi, Edwyn. Can I talk to you for a minute?' she said with halting nervousness.

"I poked my head out of the room again. 'Where's Brett? He didn't want to come?' I asked, clearly more annoyed.

"'He's home and worried about his chances,' Arlene said meekly.

"'Well, I think you just ruined his chances,' I snapped back and started to shut the door.

Arlene put her foot in the way to prevent that from happening. "'He also doesn't know I'm here. Can I talk to you for five minutes?' she said with these big, sad, soulful eyes.

"I looked her up and down and slowly released the door handle and stepped back to let her in. I shut the door as Arlene went over and sat on the couch. I sat on the armrest of the chair next to the couch. On the nightstand next to me were résumés of candidates I had met earlier that day.

"'I'll be honest. It's not just because of the stain, although the stain didn't help. I actually think another candidate is more qualified,' I told her. I picked up the stack of résumés and shuffled through them. I handed her one. 'Look at this guy. Not only is he at the top of his class, but he also knows our applications cold. He speaks four languages, too. How can Brett compete with that? I'm really sorry.'

"I got up from the chair and started to lead her to the door. She stood up and put her hands on my waist, looked me straight in the eye, and said, 'You are one of the most influential power players in New York City. You've had articles written about you in the *Wall Street Journal*, *Forbes*, *Money* magazine, and *Fortune*. Your firm has been a key moneymaker and job creator in the tristate area for the past decade, and you played an intricate part in that. Did you see the people you were speaking to today? Did you see how captivated they were with your every word? You seduced them. You seduced me. I'm not sure if you realize the effect you have on members of the opposite sex.' Arlene continued to speak as she slid her hand down to my crotch and rubbed my now-throbbing cock. I was actually hard before she touched it. I think she knew it too. This was just more proof that when you cater to a man's ego, he gets a swelled head in every sense of the word.

"She continued. 'I consider myself an attractive woman. You are a very handsome man. We are both consenting adults, and I am willing to do anything to help Brett.' Arlene finally finished, knowing this could all go very right or very wrong very quickly. I had checked her out briefly earlier, but that was all. I decided to take a few steps back to get a really good look at her body. I had never really noticed what a sexy body she had.

"'Let me ask you a question,' I said. 'If you and I were camping, and a snake bit me on the cock, what would you do?' I continued as I rubbed her shoulders. She smiled slightly because she realized at that moment she had secured the job for Brett.

"She cleared her throat and said, 'I would suck the poison out.'

"And with that, I put my fists on my hips à la Superman circa 1953 and said, 'Give me your oral presentation.'

"Arlene dropped to her knees, unbuckled my pants, slid my cock into her mouth, and sucked it hard until I came—a lot. She almost choked as what seemed like quarts of semen rolled down her throat.

"'You've made a very wise investment,' I said to her through my panting.

"'So have you,' Arlene replied while still on her knees."

⅄

Jabari stares at him in utter shock at this new revelation. He's heard the rumor of how Brett got the job but always thought Arlene had too much class to lower herself to do something like that.

"Membership has its privileges," Edwyn says, as Jabari still can't utter a word. "Do you know how many women said they slept with Clinton? Monica, Paula, and Jennifer were the top three, but there were others, many others. No one really knows how many women Clinton had. Just as no one really knows how many women I've had. Women will always be drawn to powerful men like us—him in the political world and me in the financial world." Edwyn is lost in thought about his sexual prowess.

In that silence, Jabari, still shocked, finally says, "So *that's* why she hates you."

Edwyn takes another puff of his cigar and says, "Katherine still doesn't know. Anyway, he got the job and rose through the ranks. He did better than anybody ever expected and quickly became a star. He was even better than me. As the years passed, I was given golden handcuffs. I couldn't leave because they were paying me too much, but I didn't have the authority to make any decisions. I had to go through Brett. Can you fucking believe that? The guy I brought into the firm and trained was my boss. Anyway, I knew my time was close when people started avoiding me. They would walk out of a room whenever I entered. To be treated like that after all my years there…" Edwyn's voice trails off as he stares out into space.

Jabari takes a slight step closer to him. "But it's not Brett's fault you got laid off."

Edwyn, very angry, turns to Jabari and says, "First of all, guys like me don't get laid off. We get bought out of our contracts. Second, Brett is getting paid a base close to a million dollars, and his rich father-in-law just died, leaving him millions more, giving him a nest egg bigger than my cock! Tell me how the fuck is that fair."

Jabari realizes he is losing this argument based on emotion, so he tries logic. "But isn't he a good friend of yours?" he asks, trying to get some kind of sympathetic emotion.

"I don't really give a flying fuck," Edwyn says, very indignant.

Jabari looks at him curiously and asks, "What does that expression even mean?"

"It means, if Jerry Lewis was having a telethon and he already had ninety-nine flying fucks and needed just one more for world peace and asked *me* for that one, I wouldn't give it to him!" Edwyn says, exploding in anger, resentment, and jealously.

Jabari reflects on what Edwyn says and figures there's still no reason for Brett's house to be robbed. He explains this to Edwyn as calmly as he can.

Edwyn takes in what Jabari says, turns to him, and says, "Look, I didn't want to say anything, but the club is not as profitable as it once was, and we need to cut payroll in the near future. I would hate to see you lose your job."

Jabari is a little surprised but not exactly shocked by Edwyn's statement. He just needs to be clear on this. "So if I don't rob the house, you're going to lay me off?"

Edwyn turns to him, gives a slight smile, and says, "People like you don't get laid off. People like you get fired. And in this economy, at your age, it will be very difficult for you to find another job." Edwyn moves a little closer to Jabari, who is now leaning away from him, not wanting to be so close. Edwyn continues. "You are a very trustworthy guy, and people like you. Think about it and call me later." Edwyn extends his hand. Jabari stares at it as if it were a sexually transmitted disease. "No hard feelings?" Edwyn says.

Jabari takes two steps back while still staring at his hand and says, "Edwyn, there's no feelings at all." He just stands there for a minute and finally leaves Edwyn alone with his thoughts.

⋏

Later that night, Edwyn and Katherine are having dinner, which is a very nice spread of Chilean sea bass, rice pilaf, arugula salad, and Anderson Valley Riesling white wine. Very little is said between them, as they both have a lot of things on their minds. Finally Edwyn asks, "So you're working part time? I'm surprised you were able to find a job so quickly. I guess Ernesto was able to find an opening for you?"

Katherine thinks about what kind of answer to give him and ultimately decides on one that has a double meaning. "There are lots of openings, but I chose the one with part-time hours," she says almost meekly.

"If he's HR, what do you do for him exactly?"

"I'm kind of a generalist," Katherine says, keeping the double-meaning answers open.

"So he has you in different positions?"

"Something like that," Katherine says and immediately takes a sip of wine to keep from laughing.

Edwyn has no idea what he's saying. "Listen to me," he says with a mouthful of arugula. "Just make sure he's teaching you something you might be able to use later. And don't let those limp dicks give you any shit either."

Katherine is not sure what's funnier: what Edwyn said or that he said it with a piece of arugula hanging out of his mouth. Edwyn, oblivious, looks at Katherine intently for acknowledgment.

Katherine finally responds with "I will, sweetheart."

At this time the phone rings, and Katherine immediately glances at the clock and sees it's exactly 7:30 p.m. She knows it's George, and she smiles slightly and takes a celebratory sip of wine.

Edwyn, though, is slightly annoyed the phone is ringing. He drops his fork and says, "Who could be calling us at this hour?"

Katherine, following his lead, fakes annoyance by saying, "I have no idea. I mean, really, how inconsiderate!"

Edwyn answers the phone, and Katherine watches in awe as his frown turns into a smile. "Hello? Yes! Holy shit, it's good to hear your voice too! How are you? I know. I heard you were busy. News travels fast in Gotham City. Instead of leaving you another message, I was about to throw up the bat signal. She's great! Katherine is great; thanks for asking. What's that? Dinner? Uhh, sure, that would be great idea! Talk about what now? Oh, OK, we'll talk later. Just let me know where and when. That sounds great. Go and do your thing. We'll catch up later. No, the pleasure was all mine. I'll talk to you soon. Bye." Edwyn holds the phone in his hand for a few more seconds and then hangs up. He stands by the phone with a look of satisfaction on his face.

"Who was that, sweetheart?" Katherine asks while continuing to eat.

"That was George," Edwyn says, getting excited.

"George?" Katherine says, feigning ignorance.

"Oh, you remember. He followed you like a bitch in heat at the company holiday party," Edwyn says with definitive clarity.

Then her face lights up, and he sees that she recalls. "Oh, George! How is he?" she asks, pouring it on.

Edwyn slowly walks over to her and says, "He's great. He wants to get together with me."

Katherine sees how giddy he is at the prospect of getting his old job back. "Look at you!" she exclaims.

Edwyn is now pacing the floor, thinking of the possibilities. "I think this is it. He's going to ask me to come back. He needs me back."

Katherine pours herself the last of the wine and swirls her glass. "Of course he needs you. You said Brett is busier than ever and needs qualified people to do the job. Are they going to hire an outsider they will then have to train on their systems and processes, or are they going to hire someone who practically built their systems and processes? That person is you. It has to be you." Katherine has always been great at catering to his ego, and right now she is doing a masterful job.

Edwyn gets that smug look back on his face, the one he used to wear every day when he was working. Katherine is happy to see it. "He sure does need me, doesn't he? I don't need him, but he needs me. I mean, he called me out of the blue, right?" Edwyn smiles wide and is almost dancing around the dining table.

Clearly relishing her work, Katherine says, "Look at you! I haven't seen you this excited in a long time."

Edwyn gives her a very devilish grin. "I'll show you excited," he says, and he walks over to her and drops his pants to reveal a rock-hard erection. He hasn't been this hard without medication in years. Edwyn stands there like a kid waiting to be judged on his entry in the local science fair.

Katherine switches her wine glass to her other hand, and, with her free hand, tests the rigidity of his cock. "What do we have here?" she asks in a playful way.

Edwyn now puts his hands on his waist like Supercock Man and says, "Little blue pill, my ass. What do you think of that baby?"

"Very impressive," Katherine says as she gives it a gentle squeeze to get a sense of the thickness.

He grabs her by the hand and stands her up. She takes the last gulp of wine and follows him upstairs to the bedroom.

"Let's see if I'm up to the challenge now," Edwyn says, remembering what she said earlier.

"Be gentle. It's my first time," Katherine says with a giggle.

In the bedroom, Edwyn insists on being on top. Usually Katherine prefers to be on top because she can get better leverage and the penetration is more intense. Now, she isn't sure what to expect but is pleasantly surprised as Edwyn enters her. He starts off slowly, while kissing her tenderly on the neck and earlobe. As he thrusts inside her with surprising vigor, Katherine is thinking about how the past and the present blend together. She thinks about the days when Edwyn would come home after a successful day of work, talk up a storm, eat, drink, and then they would fuck the night away. After the buyout, his libido suffered, and he was hardly interested in sex at all. Now Katherine is supposed to meet with George tomorrow night to solidify the plans to bring Edwyn back, meaning she is about to get her husband back and happy days will be here once more. The aspect of things returning to normal also excites Katherine to the point of orgasm. She climaxes and scratches Edwyn's back. Edwyn then climaxes as well. As he does so, he lets out a low grumbling moan with each thrust on an orgasm that lasts a lot longer than usual. Afterward, the beast with the two backs separates in a hot, sweaty mass. Both are panting hard and lying across each other, with the bedsheets all over the place.

"I have to say, you owned this pussy," Katherine says, goading his ego even more.

"Me? You were feral. Like a wild animal," Edwyn counters, about her masterful performance. He continues by saying, "I've been backed up. I needed that release."

Then the phone rings. For a few seconds, neither one moves. Edwyn looks up at the ceiling and says, "I think I'm blind."

Finally Katherine crawls over Edwyn to answer the phone. "Hello. Oh, hey, Jabari. Hold on; he's right here." She hands the phone to Edwyn.

He looks at the phone as if it's annoying him. He finally puts it to his ear. "Yeah, JJ. What? Not really. I came just in time. I'll be right out." Edwyn hangs up the phone; gives Katherine a kiss; and goes to the bathroom, where he puts on his bathrobe and heads out the door.

Jabari is nervously pacing the sidewalk because he doesn't live in the area and doesn't want residents to call the police on someone whom they think looks suspicious. Edwyn finally comes out of the house in a bathrobe, which is now swaying in the breeze as he walks, exposing his entire front package.

This actually makes Jabari feel more uncomfortable than being in the neighborhood. He turns his head away in disgust and says, "Really?"

Edwyn, so proud of what he has just accomplished, looks at his package and says, "Yeah. Why not? I didn't have time to put on clothes for you. "

"Me?" Jabari says.

"Sure. No offense, but you're lucky someone didn't call the cops on you. You kind of stick out around here." Of course, that's exactly what Jabari was thinking, but he would never give Edwyn the satisfaction of knowing that.

Jabari just ignores that comment and says, "I won't stay long, but I wanted to let you know that I'm in."

And with those words Edwyn can actually feel another erection coming on. He reaches to hug Jabari, but Jabari strongly pushes him away and shakes his head disapprovingly. "Please don't touch me when you are dressed like that. I'll do it, but under one condition. I plan everything. You do exactly what I say, without question, understand?"

Edwyn is giddy with laughter and starts clapping and jumping up and down like a little girl.

"And the first thing is, you're coming too," Jabari says with reserved authority.

And with that, Edwyn's laughter stops, and his eyes turn narrow. "I-I can't go. That will never happen," Edwyn says.

"Then I guess—no deal," Jabari says.

"I guess job security doesn't matter to you. What will you do after you're unemployed?"

"Well," Jabari says, taking a deep breath, "the first thing I will probably need is a recommendation. So I'll have to go to Brett's house and ask for one. When he asks why I need it, I'll tell him, Edwyn wanted me to rob your house, and I refused, so he fired me. Then I'll tell him how he got his job in the first place and see what he says."

Edwyn is shocked at hearing this. "Who the fuck do you think you are, trying to blackmail me?" Edwyn says, getting in his face.

Jabari pushes him back, saying, "What's good for the goose is good for the gander."

"What the fuck is a gander?" Edwyn asks.

"A male goose," Jabari responds.

Edwyn stands there not knowing what to say. He's been put in a very difficult position. Defeated, he tries a weak smile and says, "Look, let's try to move past this and call it even." Edwyn looks at Jabari, hoping for a nod, a smile, or something indicating that bygones are bygones.

Instead, Jabari says, "I'll call you later with more details." He starts to walk away when Edwyn steps almost in front of him and extends his hand. This handshake will solidify their commitment to this "adventure capitalism."

Jabari stares at his hand, and that is where he draws the line. "I'm not shaking the hand of a man standing in the middle of the street wearing nothing but a robe with his business swinging in the breeze." And with that, he walks away. Edwyn looks at himself, realizes how silly he looks, and heads back inside the house.

Ⴕ

Back in the kitchen, Katherine is putting ice in the last of her Glenlivet. She has a very worried look on her face, one that she hasn't had in a while. Edwyn walks in, takes a sip of her drink, and then starts rummaging through the fridge looking for a snack. He doesn't even notice her concerned look.

"Jabari will do what? What are you up to?" she asks.

Edwyn hides behind the door of the fridge as he slams his eyes shut, grits his teeth, and silently says "Fuck!" under his breath. He composes himself, fakes the biggest smile he can muster, stands up, and says, "Nothing. Just a little project I'm working on to provide for my beautiful wife." Edwyn gives her a kiss on the cheek as he takes a chair at the huge kitchen island.

Katherine sits across from him, still very concerned. "Do me a favor. Please don't do anything stupid," she says, holding her breath, hoping he will reassure her.

"Now, honey, you know me," Edwyn says with a grin and a wink.

Katherine almost recoils at the statement because that is such a loaded sentence. "It's just that I'm working on a little project too," she says as her voice softens.

Edwyn looks at her with a slight smirk on his face. Then a laugh forces its way out of his mouth. "What are you trying to do? Get me a job in human resources? Can you see me sitting at a desk talking to peons about their benefits or vacation time?" he says with clear contempt. The very thought of that causes him to laugh out loud. He gives Katherine a kiss on her forehead and then leaves the kitchen. Katherine just listens as his laughter gets softer and softer until it is all gone.

"Not exactly," she finally says.

CHAPTER 7

George has always been weak when it came to Katherine. He's always lusted after her, and when he finally got an opportunity to fuck her, he jumped at the chance. That chance encounter led to a series of moments that proved very awkward. But even with that, he still could not resist the urge to call her again.

They decide to meet at an old hotel that is set to shut down very soon. George fills out forms and reserves a room while Katherine waits by the elevator. In the room, they start to undress in front of each other without speaking. They get in the bed and start to have sex. As he fucks her, Katherine's mind is elsewhere. She is hoping this will be the last time she will have to do this. The encounter also reminds her that George is no Edwyn when it comes to sexual prowess. While Edwyn likes to move his cock in semicircles while thrusting for maximum penetration around the walls of the vagina, George is a straight in-and-out man, and, quite honestly, Katherine can't wait for him to cum. He finally does and lets out the seizure-like grunt again. As soon as it's over, Katherine motions him to roll off her. She jumps from the bed and goes to the bathroom to clean up. George just lies there as if he's waiting to be congratulated on climbing Mount Fuckerest.

Katherine comes out of the bathroom sometime later, while George prefers to lie there in the sexual afterglow. Finally, he staggers out of bed and starts to get dressed. Katherine is almost finished getting dressed and can't wait to get out of the room. She looks around as she gets dressed and notices the mold on the walls and ceiling, the faded chipped paint, and the overall lack of care. The bathroom is absolutely horrible, with dirty tiles, a leaky sink, and a toilet seat so dirty that Katherine would prefer to squat than sit all the way down. George, who is almost dressed, is desperate to break the silence and says, "Was it good for you?"

"Why'd you want to meet here? This place is a shithouse," Katherine says, ignoring George's question.

George turns to her and says, "This place is closing at the end of next month. It's been in decline for a while now, with a lack of customers, staff, and money. In fact, the only customers here are the ones who deal drugs and prostitutes. No one we know would ever come to a place like this, and, even better, the cameras in this place haven't worked in years. Besides, I have a meeting at the Sheraton two towns over, and I didn't want to chance anyone seeing us together, so—"

Katherine puts her hand up, signaling that he doesn't need to continue. "Say no more," she says, almost bored with what he has to say. "What's the status with Edwyn and the job? Where are we with that?" she asks in a very businesslike tone. She wants to remind George to stay focused on the main goal.

George glances at her for a minute, looking a little embarrassed. "Well, I have dinner with him tomorrow night and a meeting with department heads next week, which is a good sign because they agreed to talk about it with me," he tells her.

Satisfied with that answer, Katherine grabs her black trench coat and purse and heads for the door.

"You OK getting home?" George says with concern, trying somehow to give off a sense of intimacy, considering what they just have just done.

"I'll be fine. Let me know when it's done," Katherine says as she leaves.

Just as she shuts the door, she can hear George say, "Call you later?"

Katherine shakes her head.

Back inside the room, George stares out of the windows for about twenty seconds and then grabs his phone to make a call to Gilbert, his wife's nephew.

"Hello?" Gilbert says.

"Yeah, she just left. Now remember, she's a tall blonde with a black trench coat. Make it quick," George tells him.

"Does she have the pictures on her?" Gilberts asks.

"I'm not sure, but that doesn't matter. Once you take her out, I'll deal with those pictures later. Do her quietly."

"Sure thing, Uncle George," Gilbert says obediently.

"Don't call me that," George says in a testy tone.

George hangs up, rolling his eyes. Gilbert is one of those people who are too eager to please and will do almost anything to get approval from an influential family member. George has known this for years and because Gilbert has always been able to keep a secret, he's the most logical choice to deal with Katherine. He has given it a lot of thought that killing Katherine under the guise of a botched robbery in a seedy, rundown hotel seems like the best option. He already has an airtight alibi and has provided one for Gilbert and his very large sidekick, Rudy, as well. They both have everything they need to cover their tracks. He can only hope Katherine is killed quickly—and quietly.

⚔

Katherine stands in the middle of the elevator car, being careful not to let anything touch her. She briefly checks herself out in the reflection of the elevator doors when it stops on the fourth floor. She sucks her teeth and steps to the side to wait for other people to enter. The doors open, and in walks Gilbert, a rather tall and stocky individual. His face looks like that of the kind of person who would be picked last for any kind of team sporting event: surrounded by pimples and some facial hair trying desperately trying to break through the surface.

Katherine moves to the side to give him room. They smile awkwardly at each other as she moves closer to the corner, being careful not to touch it. As the elevator goes to the third floor, the doors open again.

"Shit," Katherine mutters under her breath. This time Rudy comes in. Rudy is a slender, slightly muscular black man a few inches shorter than Gilbert. He has a very serious look on his face despite the fact that he is wearing sunglasses. He walks straight toward Katherine, invading her space, forcing her to move to the front of the elevator car while he moves next to Gilbert in the back.

The doors close, and in the reflection in the mirror doors, she notices Gilbert make a head motion toward her and Rudy, nodding knowingly. Katherine is now very nervous as to what's going on. She inches closer to the door but keeps her head down and avoids direct eye contact, as the two men are now looking at her reflection.

Once the elevator reaches the lobby, she puts her hand on the door, no longer really concerned about its cleanliness. As the doors open, she bolts out and goes across the main area of the lobby. Pretending to look around, and through her peripheral vision, she sees the pair directly behind her, keeping pace. While Katherine heads to the concierge desk to buy some time, Gilbert and Rudy hang back, pretending to talk to each other and waiting to see what she does.

Katherine goes up to the woman behind the desk and sees that her name tag says Gladys. She also looks at her face and hands to get a sense of the kind of woman she is and notices her cuticles are chewed down and her hands are in desperate need of a manicure.

"Excuse me, where is your bathroom?" Katherine asks.

"Just behind you, to your left," Gladys says, pointing over Katherine's shoulder.

Katherine sprints to the restroom, which is surprisingly clean, considering the overall condition of the hotel. Once there, she cracks open the door to see Gilbert and Rudy talking to each other and pointing in her direction. Here she is in a seedy hotel with hardly any customers, cameras that don't work, and in the middle of nowhere late at night in a semiremote part of Westchester County.

"Fuck! Fuck!" She grits her teeth. She locks the bathroom door and paces, trying to figure out what do to next. She goes to the sink, turns on the water, and prepares to wash her face, but the water is a rusty, dirty color. She recoils at this because the last thing she wants to do is wash her face with dirty water. She stares at herself in the mirror, wondering how she's going to get out of this mess.

On the sink is a discarded business card for the hotel where she is. She then goes into her purse, grabs her cell phone, and sees the stun gun Ernesto gave her earlier. She now has an idea. She dials the main number for the hotel and unlocks and cracks the door ever so slightly, so Gilbert and Rudy can't see her.

Gladys answers the phone. "Westchester Hotel, how may I help you?" she asks.

Katherine has encountered a few people from Brooklyn, but she was always leery about her ability to talk with a Brooklyn accent. She's never had a lot of practice, but this is live and she is going for it.

"Yeah, howya doin', dollface," Katherine says in Brooklynese.

"I'm fine. How can I help you?" Gladys says, almost dreading the conversation.

"I need ya ta do mes a favor. I gotta date wit two dudes at your joint over dere, and I'm a little tied up at the moment, if you get the meaning," Katherine says with a slight laugh. "Anyways, I need yous ta tell dem ta get started without me, and I'll join them later."

She sees Gladys straighten her back and say, "I'm sure there's no one like that waiting for you here at this hotel."

Now that Katherine has her attention, she pours it on a little. "Sure ya do, honey. One's a tall, stocky white kid who looks like he got beat up a lot. The other is a black guy with dark glasses who's hung like a horse." Katherine sees Gladys looking right at Gilbert and Rudy.

Gladys shakes her head disapprovingly. "Yes, I see them, but we don't condone that kind of behavior at the hotel," she says sternly.

"Well, you might not condone it, but you certainly approve it," Katherine says in a matter-of-fact way.

"'Condone' and 'approve' mean the same thing, ma'am," Gladys says smugly.

"This is Gladys, right?" Katherine says, now that she has reeled her in.

"Yes. How did you know that?" Gladys says curiously.

"Yeah, da boys was tellin' me you're da frumpy, stuck-up bitch wit da horrible manicure," Katherine says, surprised by her own brashness.

Gladys instinctively looks at her hands. "Excuse me?" she replies, very offended.

Katherine says, "Yeah, da brother man says all yous need is a good fuck, an' after he's done wit me, he'll give you some of his Alabama black snake. I'll be there in ten minutes. But since you sound like you could use a good fuck, if you want him to plow you now, be my guest."

Gladys now starts pacing the floor, eyeballing the two men, who have no idea what's going on. Not wanting to raise her voice to let the other guests know what's happening, Gladys covers the phone, turns in the other direction, and, with a raised voice, says, "I know your type, and if I ever see you in this hotel again, I'll have you arrested."

At this point, Katherine comes out of the bathroom and heads toward the parking lot and says, "Good luck with that." She hangs up.

Gladys immediately hangs up and almost sprints over to Gilbert and Rudy before they can follow Katherine. They are both confused by the now-fuming Gladys. "Excuse me, but what is your business here?" Gladys says angrily.

The boys are caught off guard, never expecting to speak with anyone besides George. They stutter for a minute before Gilbert finally says, "We… uhh, we're waiting for somebody."

With that, Gladys's nose goes full flare, and her eyes widen. The vein at the top of her forehead gets thicker and thicker. "I know. She just called, and if you don't leave this hotel— and I mean right now—I will call the police and have you arrested for trespassing." Her tone and inflection cause the few customers in the lobby to stop and watch.

Now the boys are staring at each other, confused and embarrassed. Rudy takes half a step forward, and Gladys takes half a step back, remembering what she was told about him. "Wait, she called you?" he says.

Gladys points to the front door and says, "Get out. Now!" Seeing how serious she is, the boys comply without responding. Gladys looks at her hands again and realizes she does need a manicure. "Asshole," she mutters before going back to her station.

⋏

The multistory parking garage is adjoined to the hotel and looks like something out of a horror movie. It's not very well lit, there are few cars around, and the numbers indicating the floors are faded. There are staircases on the north and south sides. The men both look around on the present floor, both behind and under cars.

"Where do you think she is?" Gilbert asks, not sure what to do since he's never done anything like this before.

"How the fuck should I know?" Rudy says rather curtly. He has done this kind of thing before and is looking to get a nice fee from it. Rudy's understanding of the job is based on how quickly and quietly it is done. Also, there's an extra bonus for proper disposal of the body. He quickly looks around and knows there no way she would still be on this floor. They decide to split up. "You take that side of the floor and search here. If you see her, holler for me," Rudy says with assertiveness.

As Gilbert starts to run to the other staircase, Rudy grabs him by the arm and says, "Hey, maybe you should give me the gun, just in case."

Gilbert immediately snatches his arm away from Rudy's grasp, letting him know he is not in charge. "No. Uncle George gave it to me, so it's my responsibility. I'll search that way, and you search here," he says, looking into Rudy's eyes to show how serious he is. Rudy says nothing as Gilbert runs to the opposite end of the floor to search the other staircase.

When he is out of sight, Rudy slowly starts going up the staircase nearest to them. He gets to the next floor up and sees Gilbert on the far side, already searching under and behind cars. Rudy does the same and checks every nook and cranny on the floor to make sure they haven't missed her. When they realize she isn't on that floor, they both motion to move to the next floor.

When Rudy starts to go up the next flight of stairs, he sees one of Katherine's shoes off at the top of the staircase landing. He slowly approaches the shoe, grabs it, and nods approvingly. Rudy looks around for Gilbert, not wanting to make much noise. As soon as he turns the corner to go the next flight, Katherine charges him and gives him the full effect of the stun gun. Rudy is so shocked, all he can say is, "Ack!" as his eyes roll to the back of his head and he loses all muscle control.

Rudy falls back, hitting his head on stairs, and his body slides down to the bottom landing. Katherine slowly moves toward him and watches as foam comes out of his mouth and blood drips from the back of his head. He is motionless, and for a second Katherine is afraid. She kicks his body to check for movement. There is none. Just then Gilbert comes running over from the other side of the floor. He is pointing a silenced pistol at Katherine.

Gilbert sees Rudy on the floor. "What the fuck did you do?" he yells at Katherine. He moves closer to Rudy. "Rudy, can you hear me? Hey, Rudy," Gilbert says with great concern. His concern for his friend causes him to lower his gun on Katherine.

Katherine sees this as a window of opportunity and lunges at Gilbert, and they roll on the ground, fighting for control of the gun. She is searching for the gun's safety feature. She easily finds and activates it. Then she lets go, giving Gilbert back control.

He gets up right away, with the gun pointed at her head. "Get up, bitch," he says with authority. Katherine slowly stands up. Gilbert is smiling now, very full of himself because he thinks he is in control of the situation. "Any last words?" he says, with the gun pointed at Katherine's head.

"Go fuck yourself," Katherine says defiantly. She knows she put the safety on but is still pretty nervous.

"Fuck you," Gilbert says, squinting his eyes and wincing, indicating to Katherine he is about to pull the trigger. He does, and nothing happens. Katherine lets her body relax and gets ready to pounce again. Gilbert pulls the trigger again and again, and still nothing happens. Now embarrassed, he looks down at the gun and says, "What the fuck?"

Katherine attacks him again, and again they wrestle on the ground. The only difference now is that Katherine fights much more ferociously. She scratches at his eyes, kicks him in the groin, and bites him in several places. What gets him to release the gun is her almost biting off his ear.

"Ahhh! Fuck! Get the fuck off me!" he screams in agony, as Katherine is now in control of the gun and the situation.

She stands up fast. "Now *you* get up," Katherine says. Gilbert slowly stands up, holding what's left of his ear.

"I can't believe you fucking bit me!" Gilbert says, in clear disbelief that a plan that at first was going so right could end up going so wrong. Out of the corner of his eye, he sees Rudy move his leg a little. Gilbert leans over in his direction and says, "Rudy, get up, man. I need ya." He then turns to Katherine and says, "You can't shoot me. That fuckin' gun won't work."

Katherine gives Gilbert a steely look and says, "It does when you remove the safety catch." She removes the safely mechanism on the gun, points it at Rudy's head, and, without hesitation, pulls the trigger. Rudy stops moving. Gilbert is now in utter shock. He starts breathing very heavily as fear takes over his body. He slumps down to his knees. Katherine moves closer to Gilbert and points the gun at his head.

"Do you have any last words?" she says.

Gilbert starts crying like a little boy. He clasps his hands together in prayer to beg for mercy. "Please don't kill me. I'll do anything you want! Just please don't shoot!"

Katherine lowers the gun slightly and says, "I want three things. I want you to help me get your friend out of here. I want you to drive me to a secluded spot, and I want to know who sent you to kill me."

"I-I don't know any secluded spot," Gilbert says right away.

Katherine moves closer to him and says, "You were sent here to kill me, right?" Gilbert nods. "Take me to where you were going to dump the body. Give me your shoes and grab mine," she adds. She figures that if she needs to run or fight again, wearing more comfortable shoes would be better that the high heels she was wearing earlier.

⋏

Gilbert and Katherine carry Rudy's body down to where he has a car waiting. Rudy is placed next to Gilbert on the passenger seat, and Katherine is in the backseat directly behind Gilbert, with the gun pointed at his head. As he is driving, Gilbert has to go slowly on the turns so Rudy's head won't land on his shoulder.

Gilbert drives her to a very secluded spot on an unnamed road off of Shore Road. There is a construction site there, where Gilbert has the key to gain access. Once there, Katherine is amazed and horrified to find a hole already dug. Apparently George paid off the foreman to fill in the hole first thing in the morning, no questions asked.

"Empty your pockets. Both of you," Katherine demands. Gilbert empties his and Rudy's pockets. Apparently they were very prepared. They brought gloves and hairnets to prevent anything from linking them to the crime scene. George arranged to have their alibis confirmed weeks ago.

Katherine, now wearing Gilbert's shoes, makes him kneel in front of the hole. Because it's so cold this night and not very well lit, and because the bus stops running after a certain time, not a soul is in sight.

"Make the call," Katherine commands.

Gilbert takes out his phone and hits the predialed number. George is still back at the hotel, pacing the floor, wondering what can be taking so long. They were supposed to kill her and put the body in the hole. That way, he would have enough time to call the foreman so *he* could go to the site and cover up everything before anybody else got there. Now it's getting late, and George is hoping nothing has gone wrong. Finally the phone rings, and George jumps on top of the bed rather than go around it to answer.

"Did she give you any trouble? Did she have the pictures on her?" George says, checking his watch.

"Uhh, Uncle George?" Gilbert says nervously.

Katherine shoots Gilbert in the chest. He falls backward on top of Rudy. George, hearing the gunshot, is filled with fear and panic. He starts screaming, "Hello? Hello? Can you hear me? Gilbert?"

Katherine takes the phone out of his hand. "Hi, George," she says.

George feels weak in the knees and plops down on the bed. "Kat?"

"So it was you he was talking to in the elevator, right?" Katherine asks, putting it all together.

"You killed him," George says, gasping.

"Well, he was going to kill me first. I just beat him to it," Katherine tells him very directly.

"That's murder," George says with his voice rising.

She screams into the phone, "That's self-defense, asshole!"

George starts breathing very heavily from panic. "What about the other guy? Rudy?"

Katherine looks at the two dead bodies in the hole. "Oh, you won't see him anymore."

George gets up and is now pacing around the floor, wondering what to do. "Fuck! Fuck!" he mutters to himself.

Katherine is quite collected and focused as to what she has to do now. She has George in a corner and is more determined than ever to get what she wants. "That is an interesting word. You wanted to fuck me for a long time, and then we finally fucked. Then you tried to fuck me again, but it backfired and you got fucked. Now let's talk about Edwyn's job."

"It can't be done. They won't take him back. I already asked," George says with assurance.

"I thought you said you had a meeting with the top brass," Katherine says.

"I lied to you. They don't want him back," George says.

Katherine shifts her body weight and says, "Why not?"

George takes a deep breath, and, with halting speech says, "He was fucking up. Edwyn was making very bad decisions that cost the firm money, and I-I made the decision to fire him."

Katherine is very confused by this revelation. "You? I thought Brett was responsible for those decisions."

"He didn't want it, so I took it. I was going to do it sooner, but Brett was stalling."

"Brett?" Katherine says, very confused.

"Yeah. He tried everything to get us to keep Edwyn. He even offered to lower his own salary."

"But you wanted him gone," Katherine says.

After a pause, George says, very slightly, "Aside from Brett, we all did. It was just business."

Katherine thinks about what George has just said and remarks on how many times people have taken a situation, seen a window of opportunity that would possibly benefit them, and hurt others, all in the guise of it being "just business." When a senile millionaire signs over the fortune to a lawyer, that lawyer now has the right to take the money, right? It's just business. If an officer raids a drug den with thousands of dollars lying around, if no one is on-site, that officer has the right to help himself or herself to that money. It's better than having it locked up in the evidence room. That's just business also, right?

"Arlene fucked Edwyn to ensure Brett would get the job at the firm when he got out of school. Did you know that?" Katherine says with halting clarity.

George is stunned for a moment, because of course he knew that. Edwyn never could stop talking about his sexual conquests, particularly if one was his protégé's spouse.

But George would never admit to Katherine he knew. You never admit to something like that. "Uhhhh," George says, trying to stall for time.

"Edwyn still thinks I don't know," Katherine continues. "And Arlene didn't tell me. She didn't have to. But that was just business too. What I'm saying is, Edwyn doesn't always make the right decision. That's because he's not that bright. I've always known that. That's also why I decided to marry him. A woman who marries a man who is not that bright is making a very good strategic move. It gives her a position of dominance. She can make subtle and sometimes not-too-subtle suggestions that he will most likely claim as his own because he's too stupid to think of them himself. Personally, I like my men on the dumb side. That makes it easier for me to maneuver, operate, and negotiate."

George thinks about all she has done and said to him personally and realizes she is right. And, of course, as a man, he realizes he's been played way after the fact. "So anyway, that's why I can't get him his old job back," George says, totally ignoring and proving her argument at the same time.

"I understand. I'm going to leave now, but before I do, I'll call the police and send those pictures to your wife. Good-bye," she says, to which George feels as if he's about to have a heart attack.

"No, no, no, no. Don't do that. Here's what we can do," George says with desperation.

Katherine had no intention of doing that; she just wanted to make sure she had his complete attention.

"When are you supposed to have dinner with him?" Katherine asks.

"Uhh, tomorrow night."

"And how long do you think dinner will last?"

"I really don't know."

Katherine explodes with anger and rage. "Think, George! You have a background in fixed income and mortgage-backed securities. Now take the information I gave you, do some quantitative analysis, and give me some future projections!"

George is clearly overwhelmed and flustered. He struggles to put words together. "Uhhh, I'm not sure. I…uhh, I think."

"C'mon, George! Two hours? Two and a half hours?" Katherine says in a sadistic yet encouraging tone.

"Maybe. That sounds about right," George says meekly.

"Let's say an even three hours. Is that good?" Katherine says.

"Yes. That sounds fine," George says.

"Goody. Dinner is at eight?" Katherine says, again leading him in questioning like a child.

"Yes," George responds like a child.

"Goody again. That means dinner will officially be over by eleven. That means you have twenty-four hours, starting at eleven o'clock, to get Edwyn his old job back. And if I don't get a call from you, your fucking life is over. You will go to jail for a very long time, and I'm sure there'll be some nice bull queers who would love to make your acquaintance and get their hands on that nice, white, mushy butt of yours," Katherine tells him, borrowing a line from *The Shawshank Redemption*, which is one of her favorite movies.

"What are you doing with my wife's nephew and the other guy?" George asks.

"Nothing has changed. They told me you were going to call the foreman to fill the hole with my body, right? Well, you can still call him. In fact, I think you'd better call him."

George is silent for a moment and then asks, "Where are you going now?"

Katherine explodes with rage, yelling back at him, "Don't fucking worry about where the fuck I'm going! Do you, George, 'cause I'm doing me!"

George lets it all sink in for a minute and then humbly asks, "What am I supposed to tell my wife?"

Katherine, in a much calmer voice says, "You can't expect me to think of everything, George. Anyway, dinner is tomorrow night. Make sure you're on time, and bring your appetite." Katherine hangs up.

George sits there for a moment with the phone still to his ear, thinking and processing what has just happened. He has no idea what to do or how he would do it if he knew. He sits there for several agonizing minutes, dreading the next few moments, but he also knows that time is of the essence, as the sun will be rising in a few hours. He dials a number.

"Hello?" answers the foreman.

"It's me. You can head over there now. But instead of one body, you have to cover two," George says in a monotone.

"Two? That's not what we agreed on. It's bad enough I have the one body. For two, I have to charge you extra."

"How much?" George says, without really caring what the price is. He just wants this over.

"That's an extra five," the foreman says, half waiting for George to haggle.

"Fine. Just get it done," George says, and he hangs up before the foreman can respond.

George sits on the bed and starts asking himself questions. Can the foreman cover the bodies properly? Has he done this before? What happens when people start asking about Gilbert? What about Rudy's family? What the fuck do I tell my wife? How the fuck am I going to get Edwyn's job back? What if I get caught? What if I go to prison? Does getting fucked in the ass hurt? Is my butt really mushy?

All of this has made George extremely ill, so much so that he vomits all over the bed where he and Katherine fucked a few hours ago. Finally, after several minutes, he composes himself, even going to far as to adjust his tie, and he leaves the room and ultimately the hotel.

⋏

Katherine, however, begins to cover her tracks. She gathers everything the two men had on them, including their wallets, keys, and cash. She takes out their phones, removes both SIM cards, and bashes them to bits with rocks. Then she puts those pieces in small plastic bags that the guys also brought with them. She takes the batteries out of the phones and completely destroys them with rocks as well.

Katherine gets in Gilbert's car, and, while taking local roads back to her own car, periodically throws bits of the SIM cards out the window along with parts of the phones, as well as the men's keys. She of course pockets the cash. She's no fool. Together Gilbert and Rudy had almost $400 on them.

She decides to park on the top floor of the garage, since no one goes up there. Katherine wipes down the car of all prints using microfiber cloths they brought, takes her personal belongings, and walks away.

She gets to her car and drives home. As she is pulling in her driveway, she sees the small garbage truck owned by a private firm that her taxes are paying for. She gets out of the car, takes off Gilbert's shoes, grabs the shoes she wore, and walks over to one of the men. The man, who is a middle-aged, overweight blue-collar worker, now sees a beautiful young woman running on her sexy tippy toes, complete with red toenail polish, coming toward him. He thinks this is his lucky day.

"Excuse me. These are my husband's boots that he never wears. Can I give them to you?" Katherine says, using her damsel-in-distress voice and her come-hither looks.

"Sure thing, miss. I'll take anything you have to give me," he says, not understanding what happened earlier.

Katherine smiles brightly and then walks into her house. Once inside, she sneaks upstairs to check on Edwyn, who is drinking a glass of wine and watching a little TV.

"Hey, sweetheart. You're home late," he says, half asleep.

Katherine smiles at how grateful she is that her husband isn't more observant. "Yeah, some of the girls and I went out for a drink after work, and we lost track of time. I just have to take a shower. You go to sleep, and I'll be along in a minute," she says, like a mother checking on her child. She goes to the kitchen and begins cutting up all the men's credit cards, driver's licenses, and anything else they had on them. She puts them in the bottom of the garbage can, and when Eugenia comes in, she'll take it out.

Katherine then takes a shower to wash off the day and finally lies next to a snoring Edwyn. She is surprisingly calm despite the evening's events. She is very rational about all that has happened. She says to herself, "This whole thing started because I wanted to know what Ernesto does for a living. I had no idea George had been going there for months. I knew he was Edwyn's boss and was in a position to get him his old job back. I also knew he wanted to fuck me since forever, so of course I used what I had to my advantage. The blackmail was merely an incentive for him to move more quickly and more efficiently. I wanted to make sure I had and kept his attention. How dare he send goons to try to kill me? A relative, no less! And what was I supposed to do? You take the lesser of two evils. What would you rather have, someone trying to blackmail you or someone trying to kill you? And when someone is trying to kill you, you have two choices: give up and die, or fight to live. I chose to fight. And when the opportunity presents itself to gain the upper hand and vanquish my assassin, should I take it? Fuck yeah, I'll take it! Why not? George hired these guys and had it all arranged for me to die. He never counted on me fighting back. Tough shit! As far as I see it, I'm a victim of circumstance."

And with that, she drifts off and has the best night's sleep she's had in a long time.

CHAPTER 8

The next night she is sitting on a chair with her feet on Ernesto's desk, watching him play with the gun she fixed. He's looking at it, trying to see how she fixed it, but he doesn't want to risk taking it apart again.

She chuckles at him and says, "Would you leave that alone. You're gonna break it again."

Ernesto puts the gun down and smiles slightly. He notices her bright smile, her chipper mood, and overall laid-back posture. He doesn't know Katherine well, but he knows her well enough to know she's up to something.

"Why are you in such a good mood?" he asks very curiously.

Katherine smiles shyly and says, "My husband had a very important meeting tonight that could change a lot of things for us."

"Me too?" Ernesto asks.

"Maybe," she replies as her phone rings. Looking at it, she knows it's Edwyn. "So how did it go?"

"Fan-fucking-tastic! It went great! I think I nailed it."

"That's wonderful, honey. I'm so proud."

"I'm going out to celebrate. Don't wait up."

"Have fun."

"Honey, after tonight, things will be different from now on."

"I know they will."

"Talk later. Love you."

"Love you too."

Katherine hangs up feeling very satisfied with how things have been go-ing. To go back to how life was before is worth all the sacrifices. She is so lost in thought she doesn't hear Ernesto's question. "Sorry?" she says.

Ernesto sits up and says, "I said, what happens now?"

Katherine checks her watch, smiles slightly, and says, "Now, we wait."

"Wait for what? What are we looking for?" Ernesto says.

At this point, Katherine looks behind his shoulder at his monitors and sees someone vaguely familiar standing outside the house alone. She points to the monitor and says, "Hey. Isn't that the guy who was here before?"

Ernesto turns to the monitor. He moves in for a closer look and knows exactly who it is. "Shit. It's this asshole again. I'll be right back." He gets, and Katherine decides to walk around the floor a bit. She wanders into a bed-room where Lailani, the underage prostitute from earlier, is stitching some-thing into a trench coat. As soon as Lailani sees Katherine, she tries to hide the coat.

"No, it's OK. Let me see," Katherine says as she gently pulls the coat from Lailani's grasp. The girl finally lets go, and Katherine sees she has sewn money into the lining of the coat: tens, twenties, and a few fifties. Katherine is not sure how much money is in the coat, but apparently the girl has been doing this ever since she got to the USA. "You've sewn money in here?"

Lailani smiles and struggles to bring the words to her mouth. "Yes," she says in halting English. "I-I go home."

Katherine puts her hand on the girl's shoulder. "Good. You shouldn't be here." Katherine is generally concerned about her. She's a bitch, but not a total bitch. This girl poses no threat to her. This girl was probably stolen from or bought from her family and shipped here just so grown men could rent her by the hour to ejaculate on and in her. The point is, clearly this girl came here against her will and is just looking forward to going home. Since Katherine's life is starting to return to its former glory, she wants to try to make amends for some of the less glorious things she has done recently. She really wants to help this girl and hopes she makes it out of this place.

Meanwhile, outside, an increasingly agitated Wendell is speaking to Ernesto. Wendell has been a police officer for seven years but has been frequenting prostitutes for about nine years. He somehow finds comfort in engaging in pleasures of the flesh with women of ill repute. Ernesto has always had a habit of blackmailing people in positions of power. Police are always welcome clients because he can always use them as his personal security system to protect him against the honest cops. Usually there is little resistance when it comes to the repercussions because, as Ernesto put it, "There's so much ammo against you, you can't fight back." There's a guess that Ernesto has even more ammo against Wendell, of a literal kind, and that when backed into a corner, Wendell has no compunction whatsoever.

Wendell is shifty and pacing back and forth. Ernesto just wants him to leave. He wants to be firm, but at the same time respectful. He doesn't want to escalate things further.

"I thought I told you never to come here," Ernesto says.

"I was hoping to talk some sense into you," Wendell says as he moves uncomfortably close to Ernesto.

Ernesto takes half a step back and says, "You need to move the fuck away from me before I—"

And with that, Wendell takes out his gun and yells, "Gun!" He shoots Ernesto point-blank in the chest, and he falls down dead. He then bends down and takes another small gun from his ankle holster and places that gun in Ernesto's hands. As he takes his badge out and places it around his neck, a small band of about eight officers comes out of a van. They all have police badges around their necks and guns drawn.

"What now, sir?" says one of the officers, who is holding a battering ram and looking at the house. Wendell looks at the house and with steely eyes says, "We shut it down."

⅄

Katherine and Lailani both stand up as soon as they hear the gunshot. Katherine doesn't know where the shot came from, but she knows it was right outside the house.

"Holy fucking shit!" she exclaims as both women look very nervously at each other. Katherine leaves the room to see exactly where the police are. At the bottom of the stairs, she sees shadows and hears the commotion, the screaming of the other girls, the gasps of the johns being caught with their pants down, and the shouts from the other officers to get down on the floor and put your hands in the air. At least one officer breaks off from the rest of the group to try to find the exact location of the surveillance tapes. They know Ernesto kept tapes in his office as insurance and protection, but they're not sure where.

Katherine is now faced with a situation she's never faced before. Here she is in a whorehouse. While she isn't dressed inappropriately, wearing tight pants and a tank top, her presence there will raise questions she might not be able to answer. "Fuck! Shit!"

She has only minutes before the police come upstairs and arrest her along with the other girls. As she is scrambling to figure out a way through all this, Lailani grabs her arm and, with tears in her eyes, says, "Help, please!"

Katherine grabs her and instinctively puts her in the closet. She paces around and hears the officers getting closer.

"Most of these girls are illegal. Take them in," Katherine hears Wendell say as the officers round up the girls. As they get closer, Katherine looks at the closet door where Lailani is, then looks at her coat on the bed, and, at that moment, finds a solution. It might not be pretty, but it just might work.

When Wendell and the other officers enter the room where Katherine is, the first thing they see is her ass in the air, as she is down on all fours looking under the bed. For a moment, all of the officers lower their weapons and are stunned at this sight. "Where are you, you son of a bitch? I know you're in here!" Katherine yells as she stands up and turns around to see the officers with guns in their hands. "Oh! You scared me!" she says, visibly stunned.

"Can I help you, miss?" Wendell says, very confused but still determined.

Katherine puts her hand on her hips with equal determination. "Yes, as a matter of fact, you can," Katherine says. "You can help me find my rat bastard of a husband." She searches around the room again and sees the closet. Katherine rushes to the closet and opens the door to find a stunned and frightened Lailani. Katherine grabs her by the arm and slaps her in the face twice. "Where is he? Where's my husband? Are you the one he's been fucking? Tell me the truth!"

Lailani answers in her language. No one can understand what she is saying, but clearly she's professing her innocence and her desire to go home.

Katherine is about to slap her a third time when one of the officers comes in between them. Wendell moves toward Katherine now with his gun in his holster. He doesn't feel the woman is a viable threat. The other men follow suit. "Lady, calm down," Wendell says. "Tell me what happened."

Katherine takes a deep breath. "My husband has been acting very strange. Very cold and distant, you know? I got a phone call from his job saying he's been out sick a lot. Finally I get a few missed calls from this place, but it didn't dawn on me what was going on until I get a credit-card bill in the mail for seventy-eight hundred dollars, so I ran outta my house dressed like this to come find him, so I can kill him!" she yells and goes halfway out into the hallway. When she gets there, she screams, "I know you're in here!"

One of the officers grabs her and gently leads her back into the room. Wendell looks at her for a minute and finds her argument plausible, but he also realizes he and his crew still have a lot of work to do. "Miss, we are here on very serious business," Wendell says, taking back emotional control of the situation.

"So am I," Katherine says.

One of the officers, very confused, moves toward Katherine and says, "What a minute. How do we know you don't work here too? This could all be an act in order to avoid jail."

Yikes! Katherine realizes she has to do something and say something to get out of this room. So she uses her best assets. "Are you kidding me?" Katherine says as she unbuttons her coat to reveal her beautifully toned body. All of the officers can't help but stare. "First of all, look around you. Look at her, and then look at me. When you look at me, you want to follow me into the bedroom. When you look at her, you want to follow the Ho Chi Minh trail. Second, if you were married to a woman like me, would you come to a place like this?"

The officer is momentarily stunned and can only mutter, "Uhhh..."

Now she moves in for the kill. "Exactly," Katherine says, her voice cracking. "What am I going to do? Do you know how embarrassing this is for me? I have done everything he has asked me to do. Even things I can't discuss here with you fine officers. I-I..." Katherine lets herself go and lets the tears flow. She collapses in the officer's arms, and he's not sure how to handle this kind of situation. He desperately looks to Wendell to throw him a lifeline or something. The officer is now very embarrassed at what he said and wishes he could take it back.

Wendell orders one of the officers to take Lailani out of the house and put her in the van with the other girls. She is still protesting her innocence and also that Katherine is wearing her trench coat, but since no one understands her, her words are literally falling on deaf ears.

Wendell then moves closer to her and says, "What's his name?"

Katherine says, "Well, I'd rather not say because he's a highly visible partner at a law firm in midtown. If word got out that he was picked up, the scandal to him, the firm, our children would be—"

Wendell cuts her off. "And you want to try to keep it quiet." Katherine nods. "Look, I'm sure you're a wonderful wife," he continues, "but we are here on official business to shut down the guy who runs this joint and make sure this operation is dismantled forever. I can't go into all that we found here, but all you need to know is, when we do find your husband, we will be very discreet with him. No one needs to know about his business here."

Katherine takes a deep sigh of relief and takes his hand. "Thank you. Thank you so much, officer. I really appreciate it. I'm going to go now so you officers can finish your work."

The first officer who accused her of being a hooker now steps forward and says, "I can drive you home, miss, if you want."

Wendell gives him a very disapproving look, and the officer shrugs.

Katherine smiles slightly, puts her hand on the officer's face, and says, "You're very sweet, but I think I'll walk home." She starts to leave and then stops for a second and looks at Wendell.

After a few minutes, Wendell says, "What's the matter?"

Katherine takes a step back and says, "I know you. The guy who owns this place mentioned you. I saw a video of you in the office. He was talking about how he was planning on blackmailing you to make sure his shop stayed open. Is that why you're here?"

All of the officers stop and stare at Wendell, whose eyes are fixed on Katherine's.

"Is that what he told you?" Wendell says in a cold voice.

"He showed me the video of you and one of the girls," Katherine adds.

"First of all, are you sure it was me? You shouldn't speculate on things you aren't sure of. Secondly, we've been watching this guy for quite a while. Looking at people going out and coming in, and I know this guy has blackmailed people over the years. Good people with good families. Some of these people are very prominent in this city in the way of politics and law enforcement. People who might not be perfect, but they don't deserve to be treated like common criminals. He's made a lot of enemies, and that's why I'm here. To put an end to this. I don't know what you saw, but I'm pretty sure it wasn't me. I know he taped other people, and those tapes are here somewhere. Those people would prefer not to let those secrets out."

"It looks like we both have secrets to keep. But what are you going to do with all of those tapes?" Katherine asks.

"Don't you worry. When we're done, there will be no trace of anything," Wendell says. He puts his hand on her shoulder. "Go home now."

And with that, Katherine buttons her coat and slowly makes her way down the stairs. As she descends the staircase, Wendell yells, "Civilian coming down! Do not engage!"

Katherine passes several officers, all with guns in their hands. She wonders what kind of material Ernesto had on Wendell. Whatever it was, it was worth killing over. She passes the last officer and steps outside. The cold air hitting her face is a welcome relief. There are more cops positioned on the other side of the front gate, one of whom seems strangely fixated on her.

"You sure you don't need a ride, miss?" says a young officer, who looks as if he has just gotten out of the academy.

"No, thank you," Katherine says as she walks away. She turns back once and sees the officer is still looking at her. She doesn't even bother getting in her car for fear of the officer insisting he drive her home. She can't chance them finding out where she lives and realizing she lied her ass off to get out of that house.

As she walks off into the night, she dries her tearing eyes and smiles slightly and chuckles at how easy it was for her to get out. Being exceptionally beautiful does have its advantages. Men always let beauty cloud their judgment even if they don't mean to. It's one of the oldest pieces of knowledge that has lasted throughout the ages. She used her two best weapons: her body and tears. Any argument a man makes using logic and rationalization is thrown out the window once he sees a woman cry. It makes him weak, and he lowers his defenses and is open to every possible attack from a female. The roughest, toughest man in the world will crumble like a house of cards when the faucets start to flow.

Compounding the bullshit story Katherine has told is the damsel-in-distress syndrome. That's when the men try to be chivalrous and save the woman from a perilous situation. Why? Because they are men, and men seem to think they are the only ones who can improvise and get out of a sticky situation using their talents. On top of that, she took that girl's trench coat with money sewn inside! How ballsy was that! Although she feels bad for the girl, the good news is she will be deported, which is what she wanted in the first place. The money would most likely be confiscated and put in an evidence room, or some cops with sticky fingers would help themselves to it.

Katherine says to herself, "Things have fallen very well into place. I got out of a tough jam with a new coat filled with money, and Edwyn is well on his way to getting his old job back, thanks to George and me. I'm hungry, and when I get home, I need to take a shower and make myself a peanut-butter-and-honey sandwich."

And with that, Katherine walks off into the night—victorious.

Chapter 9

Edwyn is driving down the street to pick up Jabari, saying the same thing over and over in his mind. "This is it! This is it! Tonight is the fucking night!" Edwyn is dressed in all black, including a black cap. He sees Jabari standing at a bus stop wearing the exact same thing and carrying a backpack. Excited now, Edwyn smiles broadly as he pulls over to the stop, and Jabari gets in.

Once in the car, Jabari notices the stupid grin on his face. "Don't smile like that," Jabari says dryly.

Too excited to contain himself, though, Edwyn starts hitting Jabari on the arm and yelling, "Tonight is the fucking night! This is it!" While Edwyn is giddy like a schoolboy, Jabari is much more serious. A man on a mission, he is pensive and looks very determined.

"You ready?" Jabari says.

"Yes," Edwyn says. "But I need to make a phone call first." He takes out his phone and starts dialing.

As he does, Jabari says slyly, "Shouldn't you be hands free?"

Edwyn gives him a sharp look for trying to admonish him.

Katherine picks on the other line. "So how did it go?"

"Fan-fucking-tastic! It went great! I think I nailed it."

"That's wonderful, honey. I'm so proud."

"I'm going out to celebrate. Don't wait up."

"Have fun."

"Honey, after tonight, things will be different from now on."

"I know they will."

"Talk later. Love you."

"Love you too."

And with that, Edwyn hangs up, and Jabari gives him a very curious look and asks, "Who did you nail this time?" He is insulting him and alluding to his sexual prowess at the same time, hoping he won't notice.

"Never mind that. It's time to get serious," Edwyn says very seriously.

Jabari looks at Edwyn again and sees he is much more serious tonight. Edwyn has his game face on. Jabari gets serious as well. This is a very big night for both of them.

Jabari looking straight ahead and says, "Don't worry about me. I know what I'm doing."

Edwyn glances at him, smiles slightly, and says, "Really? So you *are* your father's son."

"Stop the car," Jabari says with all seriousness.

"What?" Edwyn says, very confused. "Why?"

Jabari glares at Edwyn, slaps the dashboard, and yells, "Stop the fucking car!" He then opens the door while the car is still moving, leaving Edwyn no choice but to stop the car.

Once the car stops, Jabari gets out and slams the door shut, and Edwyn finally realizes there are things he really should not say to people. He knows that Jabari's father is a very touchy subject.

"What's wrong?" Edwyn asks while rolling the car windows down and moving alongside Jabari.

Jabari keeps his eyes straight ahead and says, "If we do this, no more talk about my father! Never! No more! Understand? Not one fucking word!"

Edwyn, hoping to placate him, stops the car, gets out, and runs in front of him to prevent him from walking any farther. "You're right," Edwyn says. "Your father's death was—"

"Your fault!" Jabari says, cutting him off. "Say it! Say it now, or I walk!" Jabari is looking him so intently in the eye, it makes Edwyn very uncomfortable. Edwyn has never thought about the pain Jabari Sr.'s death has caused his son.

"Your father's death was my fault," Edwyn says, somewhat ashamed. He's never said it out loud before.

"You're going to have to do better than that," Jabari says, clearly not satisfied and wanting to put Edwyn on the spot some more.

Edwyn takes a deep breath and says, "Your father, under my instruction, committed a criminal act and, as a result of that act, was killed. I told him it was an easy job, and he believed me, and I actually knew there would be risks. I betrayed his trust, and he died because of me." Edwyn reflects on what he has said, and seeing the hurt in Jabari's eyes for the first time brings real tears to his own.

Jabari is unmoved. "This job is a one-time deal. If you can't get your shit together after this, you need to get a real job. You hear me, Eddie?" Jabari tells him.

Even though they are on a job together, Edwyn still doesn't like being called Eddie and still wants to let Jabari know who's in charge. "Don't call me Eddie," Edwyn says, trying to be serious and take back the situation.

"I'm not fucking joking," Jabari says.

And with that, Edwyn lets him run the show and operation. "Deal." Edwyn sticks out his hand to seal the deal, but Jabari looks at his hand, looks at him, and heads back to the car.

Edwyn stares at his hand a little bit and then heads back to the car. Once in and back on the road, Edwyn begins thinking—thinking about the last time Jabari actually shook his hand. He knows it was before his father died but can't remember when they stopped. He wants to ask Jabari about it but doesn't because it seems inappropriate.

They stop in front of the house, and Jabari motions for him to head to the side street. "You sure this is a good spot?" Edwyn asks.

Jabari nods and says, "This is fine. Right here is good. Keep the engine running. Do not get out of the car unless I call you."

Edwyn is not a little hunched over the steering wheel and breathing very heavy. His hands are also shaking as he says, "I don't want to use my phone. They might be able to trace it."

Jabari takes out a pair of two-way radios and hands one to Edwyn. "I'll call you with this."

Edwyn takes the two-way and holds it lovingly. "You *have* thought of everything," he says without looking at Jabari. When he finally does look at him, he sees Jabari is very upset. "You're not having second thoughts, are you?" Edwyn asks with concern.

Jabari finally looks at Edwyn and says, "I still don't understand why you are doing this. They are very nice people, her father just died, and now they're trying to have a baby…"

"There's not going to be a baby," Edwyn says, almost deadpan.

And with that, Jabari stops talking, stops concentrating on anything but what Edwyn has just said. He knows there's more to the story and is now waiting for the rest.

Edwyn tries not to look Jabari in the eye, but every time he glances in Jabari's direction, those big brown eyes are staring right at him. He takes a deep and then lets it out. "I told you Arlene and I fucked, right? Well, you know happens when two people fuck, right? When she told me she was pregnant, I couldn't believe it. At first, she was thinking about keeping it, but I was convinced the scandal would be too much for us to handle. We got a referral from a guy at the club who'd dealt with this kind of thing before. Anyway, the moron fucked up the D&C and scraped so much against her uterus, she can't hold an egg. She will never be able to have children."

Jabari stares at him with his mouth half open in utter disbelief. The little respect he had for Edwyn has gone right out of the window.

Edwyn has never told another soul about what happened. That has always been between him and Arlene. They swore to go to their graves with that secret. When the time came, Arlene would make up a story to Brett and maybe suggest adoption. Now, Edwyn is sitting there waiting for Jabari to say something, anything, like, "Oh, I'm sure you did the best you could." Or "I would have done the same thing if I were in your shoes." Jabari is just staring out of the window in dead silence.

Finally, Jabari puts on a pair of black gloves, turns to him, and says, "Here we go." As he starts to get out of the car, Edwyn grabs his arm to stop him. Jabari doesn't want to look in his face anymore, but he slowly turns to face

Edwyn's sad eyes. He looks like a dog that just shat on the rug but still wants you to tell him it's OK and he's still loved, wanted, and needed.

Instead, Jabari says nothing, to which Edwyn extends his hand and says, "Good luck."

Jabari just stares at his hand, and Edwyn is a little annoyed. "Why is it you won't shake my hand? I can't remember the last time you shook my hand. Shake my hand now," Edwyn demands.

"You forced and literally fucked your protégé's wife as a bribe to make sure he got the job at your firm. She got pregnant, had an abortion at your insistence, and, as a result, will never be able to have children. You are now forcing and figuratively fucking someone else to rob the house of your protégé and his wife, which you feel has riches inside left by your protégé's father-in-law, who only recently died, and you want me to shake your hand? Is that for validation, domination, or indignation?" Jabari says with surprising attitude while staring him in the eye.

Jabari then gets out of the car and heads toward the house.

Edwyn stares out of the driver's side window, wondering about the choices he's made in his life. More importantly, he is wondering how his choices have gotten to this point in his life, where he has to resort to robbery to make ends meet. As he wonders this, he can hear the faint sound of glass breaking. Now focused on the house, he is ready for action. Knowing that Jabari will come out of the house any moment now with a bag full of cash and other valuables, he holds the steering wheel tight and presses on the accelerator. Suddenly there is a crackling sound coming from his radio.

"You there?" Jabari says in a very faint whisper.

"Yeah. You coming out soon?" Edwyn responds, also whispering and getting nervous, hoping that nothing is wrong.

"You weren't kidding when you said this guy was loaded. There's millions here," Jabari says matter-of-factly and surprisingly upbeat.

"Millions?" Edwyn says with excitement. He looks at his crotch and grins as an erection starts to form.

"There's a lot of cash around and expensive jewelry. But you didn't say anything about the gold. We may have to renegotiate our agreement," Jabari says.

"Gold?" Edwyn says, now fully erect.

"Yeah. There are at least four gold bars up here. But there's no way I can carry all this by myself. You have to help me," Jabari tells him. And with that, Edwyn slowly loses his erection. This is a development he didn't anticipate.

"I can't," Edwyn says, almost pleading, not wanting to get actively involved. It's just one of his rules—not to get his hands dirty if he can hire someone to do it for him.

"Well, I guess we'll have to abort for now and come back another time, because I can't carry all of this by myself. I'll be out in two minutes," Jabari says finally.

"No!" Edwyn shouts before catching himself and lowering his voice. "Are you sure you can't carry some of it and maybe make two trips?" Edwyn asks as a last-ditch effort.

"Listen. Why do this in two trips when you and I can do it in one? Besides, taking two trips would be too risky. I might be seen, and we wouldn't want that, would we?" Hearing no response, Jabari asks again, "Edwyn, would we?"

"No, I guess not," Edwyn says very softly.

"I consider myself a strong man. Now, if I'm saying this is too much for me to carry, it's got to be a lot. You have to come up."

There is dead silence on the other end of the line, and finally Edwyn says, "I-I'll be up in a minute."

"No. Not a minute, now," Jabari says and then turns off his radio before Edwyn can respond.

Edwyn looks down at his crotch and thinks his penis has actually shrunk in size. "Shit!" he finally says before getting out of the car. He stands there for a few seconds to muster the courage and then goes to the back of the house.

The back door opens easily enough, and he walks through the kitchen, where he looks at the kitchen island and sees an empty wine glass and a broken bottle of red wine on the floor. The wine has made a huge stain in the kitchen. Edwyn doesn't really dwell on that as he moves onward. He moves toward the living room, where a television program about babies is playing on mute in the background and Arlene is sleeping in the chair. On the nightstand next to her is an open bottle of antidepressants. Edwyn gets a closer look at her and strokes her face with the back of his hand and smiles slightly. He also notices the trail of blood. It starts from the back of the house, stops where Arlene is, and then continues upstairs. Edwyn strokes her hair again before moving to the upstairs bedrooms. As he leaves, Arlene wiggles a few of her fingers, but Edwyn doesn't take notice.

As Edwyn moves up the staircase, he notices blood smears on the walls, and the trail of blood continues on the second floor. Jabari never mentioned seeing any blood, and he never mentioned bleeding. Once he gets to the second landing, the first thing Edwyn sees is Brett lying on the floor with a shotgun next to him. His left hand is also bleeding profusely. Edwyn starts to think maybe Brett has bled to death and he's now an accessory.

Edwyn continues moving down the hallway looking for Jabari and enters the master bedroom. The room is very large, with the standard fare: a king-size bed, ornate ceiling fan, huge walk-in closets, and, what really piques his interest, a huge armoire. It's made of cherry wood and houses a huge flat-screen television. The storage drawers underneath that usually house DVDs, some books, and a small collection of porn are actually a fake panel that opens up to hide the safe. The safe door is wide open, revealing cash with a black bag on the floor beside it. Edwyn counts it with his eyes and sees only about five thousand dollars. Confused, he almost sticks his head in the safe to see if he missed something.

"Where the fuck is the rest? Where's the gold?" Edwyn says, very confused and slightly perturbed.

He sticks his head out the bedroom door to look for Jabari, wondering where hell he went. He pauses for a minute and then makes the decision that the money in the safe is better than nothing and that he doesn't want to leave empty-handed, so he haltingly puts the radio on the edge of the bed and moves toward the safe to start filling the bag with loot. The radio is so close to the edge of the bed that it falls on the floor, and Edwyn jumps out of his skin.

"Shit!" Edwyn says.

He turns back to the safe and is concentrating so intently on filling the bag that he hardly hears the faint sound of police sirens. Now done, he stands up and scans the room to see if there's anything else he can take before he leaves. It is now that he hears the sirens, but it doesn't quite register with him yet. He's thinking maybe it's a fire truck and there's a fire somewhere.

As the sirens get louder, though, he can clearly tell this is a police car and not a fire truck. And with that, Edwyn runs downstairs and straight for the front door. The only thing that stops him is the sight of Arlene, fully conscious and very confused. The sight of her makes him drop the loot bag with a thud. She holds her forehead as if to contain a splitting headache. She's dizzy and is having trouble focusing, but seeing Edwyn in her house gives her heightened clarity. She knows something is going on, and, with Edwyn in her house, with their history, she is filled with rage, and she lets him know it.

"What the fuck are you doing in my house?" she barks at him. Edwyn just stands there, not sure how to answer. Arlene looks at the bag, points, and says, "What the fuck is in that bag? Where's Brett?" she yells at him. Edwin's still not saying anything, and Arlene gets in his face and says, "Where the fuck is my husband?" Knowing this could end badly and not knowing what else to say, he pushes Arlene out of the way and heads for the door. Arlene regains her footing and takes off after him.

⚔

Out on the front yard, the first units are responding to the scene. And what a scene it is. Edwyn is trying to make it to his car but is not even close, as Arlene tackles him to the ground and proceeds to pound his face with a series of punches and scratches. All of the rage Arlene has had against Edwyn over the years she takes out on him at this moment. Both officers are trying to pull Arlene off him. They manage to do so very briefly, but Arlene wiggles out of their grasp and kicks and scratches Edwyn some more. A second car responds to the scene. Two more officers get out, and it takes all four officers to get Arlene off of Edwyn. Even then, the officers have trouble holding her back, and she kicks at and even spits in Edwyn's direction. They finally get her to calm down, assuring her that he will face the full penalty for every law he's broken.

Now very defeated and with a face full of scratches, kicks, and punches, Edwyn is read his Miranda rights.

As he is put into handcuffs, Edwyn sees a car coming through the intersection. At first it goes at normal speed, but soon it slows down as the occupants notice the commotion. Edwyn wonders if someone in that car knows him. The thought of someone seeing him like this is too much for him to bear, and he turns away from the car in complete and utter embarrassment.

The officers finish placing the cuffs on him and usher him into the patrol car. Edwyn looks out of the corner of his eye and sees the car slowly drive away. As Edwyn is being driven to the police station, many questions run through his mind. How did the cops get here? Who called them? Where the fuck is the rest of the money Jabari said was in the house? And last, Where the fuck is Jabari?

These questions, of course, might never be answered, but suddenly more relevant questions start running through his mind. Namely, Will I go to jail, and if so, for how long? And finally, Will I get fucked up the ass, and will it hurt?

As he reaches the police station, Edwyn shudders in fear and starts to get very nervous. The reason is because those latter questions will eventually be answered. It's just a matter of time.

CHAPTER 10

Fingernails. It's amazing how many fingernail bits and pieces can accumulate from ten fingers. Some of the nails came off the finger whole, and others had to be broken in several pieces. He has been picking at his fingers so long that some of them are starting to bleed. Edwyn's been in that room at the police station long enough, his nails might grow back so he can bite them off again.

Usually police use the same tactic when questioning a suspect. They bring the suspect into the interrogation room first and leave him or her there for a while. Initially, the suspect is confident, almost cocky with an alibi, thinking he or she is ready for any questions the police will have. As time passes, the suspect becomes less confident and starts to consider other variables he or she hasn't thought of before, mistakes the police have probably picked up on. This goes on until so much time has passed that the suspect thinks the police already have the proof to get a confession, conviction, and prison sentence.

The method here was very different. The police brought Edwyn in and asked some questions first. Edwyn told them the botched robbery was all Jabari's idea, and he was forced to come along under the threat of violence. The police left a few minutes later and haven't been back since. That was almost ninety minutes ago. They did give him his phone call, and Edwyn called his house. It went to the answering machine, which is strange because Katherine should have been home already. She didn't say anything about going out again. What could she be doing?

In any event, Katherine will hear the message and come to the police station with the lawyers to release Edwyn from police custody so they can return home and plan a defense strategy.

Finally, the interrogation room door opens, and Detectives Clark and Johnson come in. They are dressed very sharp and enter the room with confidence. Edwyn notices Clark is carrying a folder. Clark gently puts the folder in the center of the table. Edwyn at first is not sure what to say. He doesn't know if he should ask about the folder or ask if the officers have spoken to someone to corroborate his story. He decides to go with the latter.

"Did you speak to Gorman? He told you I was set up, right?" Edwyn says with a slight cockiness, hoping his status will give him a few cards to play.

The room itself is only eight by eight, which is on the small side. The reasoning here is that the person being questioned might feel that in a room as small at this, the walls are closing in. The table where Edwyn is sitting is right in the middle facing the door. Despite the size, Johnson and Clark work the room like pros. Both men are standing in front of Edwyn, with Johnson standing behind Clark, a little off to the side. Johnson starts to walk toward him and says, "Very briefly. But let's go back a bit with your story. You said this was all *his* idea."

Clark chimes in and says, "'Him' as in Jabari Douglas Jr., right?"

Edwyn thinks for a minute to make sure he told them the proper story. He says, "Yes. That's right. Did you speak to him? Did you bring him in?"

"Yes," Johnson says, "he's being questioned now by Gorman."

Edwyn now says with conviction, "He told me to rob the house, and I would be the getaway driver." Both detectives look at each other very curiously. Edwyn catches that look and continues. "It's true. He told me to do it."

"Why would you agree to that?" Clark asks.

"Well, mainly because he threatened to kill my wife if I didn't go along with his plan," Edwyn says, almost nervously. "I couldn't do that to her. How would she defend herself? A rough, dark-hearted man who's probably capable of animalistic violence against my innocent wife? I mean, how would she be able to defend herself?"

Johnson now steps forward and says, "You mentioned the two of you communicated with a two-way radio. Where is that radio now?"

Edwyn thinks back to earlier in the night. I know I put it on the bed, and it somehow fell off. Then I heard police sirens and ran for the door. Did I take the radio with me, or did I leave it in the house? Shit! I can't remember! Where the fuck is Jabari? I bet he knows. "I must have lost it," he says finally.

"Well, that's convenient," Johnson says.

"As standard procedure, we did a check on Jabari Jr.," Clark says. "He has no criminal history whatsoever, not even a parking ticket."

"Well, that doesn't prove anything. He could have just covered his tracks very well. You know, some of those people are pretty slick while evading the police," Edwyn says with raw arrogance.

The detectives glance at each other again. "Those people?" Clark says, looking for clarification. He looks at Johnson and really wants to explore that statement, but Johnson, using facial expressions, tells him not to dwell on it. Instead, he should just stay on task. Johnson doesn't need any inflammatory comments to nail this guy. He has all the ammo he needs right in that folder. They have been partners for a long time and play off each other very well.

Johnson tosses the folder on the table and leans on the table with his fists, standing over Edwyn. "We did, however, come across a Jabari Sr., and he had a lengthy criminal record." Johnson opens the folder, which has pictures of Jabari Sr. at different ages in his life. He spreads them out on the table so Edwyn can get a better look at them.

Edwyn touches a few. He never realized how many times Jabari Sr. was actually arrested until seeing those various mug shots from different periods in his life.

"I guess he wasn't as slick as some of those other people," Clark says.

Edwyn puts his head down now, too embarrassed to respond.

"Most of the arrests have been B&E in suburban areas," Johnson says.

"Just like this one," Clark adds. "You know what's interesting about these arrests?"

Edwyn's throat suddenly gets very dry. His face feels very flush, and he has an urgent need to pee. "W-What's interesting about that?" he finally spits out.

"After his initial arrest, the person who picked him up or bailed him out wasn't his wife or his son. It was you," Clark says.

"It was always you," Johnson adds.

Both Johnson and Clark are standing on opposite sides of the room, with Edwyn in the middle. This forces Edwyn to look at both of them in different directions every time they speak, much like a tennis match.

Clark grabs some of the arrest reports and starts flipping through them. "You came and got him almost every time. Why would you do that?"

"I guess he was too embarrassed to call anyone else. He wanted to keep it very quiet, so instead of calling family, he called me. What was I supposed to do? Of course I went and bailed him out," Edwyn tells the detectives.

"Or maybe because you orchestrated most of the crimes, you felt obligated to bail him out, mainly to protect yourself," Johnson says.

"No, no," Edwyn says. "Jabari Sr. planned most of the crimes all by himself."

Johnson and Clark now move closer to him as if going in for the kill. "But now you're saying Jabari Jr. forced you to commit this robbery?" Johnson says.

"He said he would kill me," Edwyn says right away, needing something for them to focus on.

"First you said he was just going to kill your wife. Now it's you and your wife? Which one is it?" Clark says right away.

Edwyn is not sure how to respond to that and tries to think of an answer.

Johnson, disrupting Edwyn's thought process, says, "Mr. Kinney says he saw a man in his house—"

"He saw a black man, right?" Edwyn says, interrupting him, hoping to turn the tide to his favor.

"Actually, that's not what he said," Johnson says. "He says it was a middle-aged white male. He couldn't make out the face completely because of the distance, but he could swear it almost looked like Bill Clinton. Now, I remember when he was in the White House, and people would jokingly refer to him as the first black president, but that doesn't really make him black, does it?"

Edwyn now realizes all of that talk about him emulating the look and sexual legacy of Bill Clinton might not have been a good thing after all.

"Well, that doesn't matter," Clark says. "Mrs. Kinney got a good look at your face when you ran down her stairs, and you do have a white face."

Edwyn isn't sure about how to respond to that.

Johnson doesn't give Edwyn a chance to answer. "And when she was questioning you as to why you were in her house in the first place, you ran right past her and out the front door. First officers on the scene reported Mrs. Kinney had wrestled you to the floor."

"Yeah, I heard she beat the shit out of you. Any response to that?" Clark adds with a slight chuckle.

Edwyn is very flustered and not sure what to say. He takes two deep breaths as the detectives look at each other. "Look, like I told you before," Edwyn tries to begin again.

Clark now takes a seat next to Edwyn. "When the officers went to Jabari's house, he was just about sit down with his wife for a late dinner. He said something to the officers that made them wonder about his involvement. And it certainly made us wonder about yours."

Johnson takes the seat on the other side of Edwyn, directly across from Clark. "His wife cried hysterically when those officers insisted that Jabari come down to the station for routine questioning. Trust me. They had no clue what was going on." Johnson pauses briefly and then continues. "We have a theory on what happened. You want to hear it?"

"I think you know where we're going with this," Clark chimes in.

"Stop me if you've heard this one," Johnson says, staring directly in Edwyn's eyes. Johnson takes a deep breath.

At this point, Sergeant Gorman walks into the room. He is middle aged, with a weather-beaten face that reflects great concern. Edwyn is very relieved to see Gorman because he knows there's still a chance he can get out of this. Over the years, Edwyn and Katherine have contributed to the local police department with very generous donations. These donations have translated into special privileges that Edwyn and Katherine have been able to enjoy thoroughly, such as the time Edwyn was pulled over because he was driving erratically as a result of having one too many. Edwyn showed the officer a special pass given to him by Gorman, and the officer never said another word except for "Have a good night, sir."

One of the closest calls was one night when he was coming home from a company-related after-party event and got into an accident with another car. Apparently he lost control of the car and slammed into a man driving a brand-new BMW. Edwyn had a very good reason for losing control of the car that night: he was in the midst of an explosive orgasm, courtesy of a woman who was not his wife. The woman was won at an auction sponsored by a "local talent agency" that catered to the financial industry. The last two contestants were George and he. Brett could not bother with such, in his words, ridiculousness. George wanted nothing more than to ape-cum all over that girl's chest and face. George lost out, not because he didn't have enough funds to procure the woman. He conceded mainly because Elizabeth was supposed to be away that weekend, but the trip was canceled and he now had no fucking venue. Katherine, however, was on a weekend retreat and spa in Vail, Colorado. And for $3,500 a day, she wasn't going to leave that place unless it literally caught fire.

Edwyn had given the woman who was his prize strict instructions regarding fellatio in the car. Under no circumstances should any bodily fluid touch his suit, which cost an estimated $5,500. That meant not one drop of her saliva and certainly none of his semen could touch any part of his suit. And she was a true professional, having the ability to make him orgasm within four minutes (yes, he timed her), while Edwyn was driving at two thirty in the morning, going at least seventy miles per hour, having had one too many, and having cocaine in his system. There was no way he would have been able to give his full attention to driving. Something had to give. The driver of the BMW was very lucky he wasn't killed, considering the damage to his car, which was absolutely destroyed. Edwyn had to buy the silence of the driver with a settlement. The police said they would take care of everything if Edwyn made a sizable donation to fix the roof of the police headquarters, which was damaged from a storm the year before. Five months and $50,000 later, all was well. Edwyn was never charged in the crash, he never heard from or saw the driver again, and the roof was repaired. It was a win for all involved.

But now the look on Gorman's face told Edwyn this might cost a little more than $50,000. "Jack! Jack!" Edwyn says, rising to meet him while extending his hand for a handshake. Gorman starts to shake his hand and then stops and slowly lowers it, leaving Edwyn standing embarrassed and adding even more awkwardness and tension to a situation that already has too much of both. Edwyn finally lowers his hand and sits down, dejected. He was hoping that if Gorman at least took his hand, there might be a glimmer of home that he would have an ally. But with Gorman's action, Edwyn is slowly starting to realize he is totally alone.

"I wish I were here under different circumstances, Edwyn. But this is a pretty serious situation we're dealing with," Gorman says with sudden frankness.

Edwyn adjusts himself and begins as he always does, by buttering people up. "Jack," he begins, "we've known each other for a very long time, and I have contributed to the local police as well as this precinct in particular. I have always had the highest respect for you and your men. Having said that, I know this looks bad, and this might not paint me in the most positive light. But there is a lot more to this story than it seems. As I was saying to your men, Jabari was behind—"

"I just finished speaking to Jabari," Gorman says, interrupting him. "Do you know what he told me? He told me this whole thing was your idea. He says you were going to fire him from the country club if he didn't go along with your plan, even after you promised his father on his deathbed you wouldn't. He also told me you were the one who got his father killed. He reiterated again that this entire idea of breaking into your protégé's home to steal what you thought were millions was yours from the very beginning." Gorman stops to let that all sink into Edwyn's head.

"And why would I do that? What purpose does it serve for me to do that?" Edwyn says with slight indignation.

"He says you blamed Brett for getting fired from your job," Gorman says.

"It was a buyout!" Edwyn blurts out, screaming. He says it so instinctively, he doesn't even think about it. Gorman and the other officers look at one another with shock and surprise. Clark tries to hide his smirk. As Edwyn is examining their looks, it seems as if they were expecting him to say that. They must have known how much he hates that common term "fired." "At this point, it doesn't matter what it was," Edwyn continues. "Are you going to believe me or him? Are you really going to take his word over mine?"

Gorman takes out a small tape recorder and sets it on the table. Edwyn is a little surprised to see it and is thinking they have taped this whole conversation. "In this case, I will definitely take your words." Gorman hits Play, and Edwyn's mouth drops open. He recognizes this as the conversation he and Jabari had that night at the club. He watches the officers' faces as they listen to his voice as he basically threatens to fire Jabari if he doesn't go along with the plan to rob Brett's house.

Gorman stops the tape. "Did you know Jabari was recording you?" Gorman asks, which is essentially a rhetorical question because obviously Edwyn had no idea that exchange was being taped. If Edwyn knew, he never would have said anything at all. Or at least you would hope so.

"W-Where did you get this from?" Edwyn asks with trepidation.

"Jabari brought it in with him," Gorman says.

Johnson and Clark move closer to Gorman. "That's good stuff," Johnson says with intrigue.

Clark follows up by saying, "You got any more where that came from?"

Gorman looks at the two officers and then trains his eyes on Edwyn, and the other officers do the same. Edwyn now gets that sinking feeling that as bad as the first clip was, this next one will most likely doom him.

"Actually, I have something you really should hear," Gorman says with resignation, knowing this piece of evidence will doom a man he once called a close friend.

As Gorman plays the tape and the other officers listen to it, Edwyn is not paying attention to what was said but rather where it took place. The clip is from when Edwyn admitted to Jabari that his actions got Jabari Sr. killed.

Edwyn thinks, how can this be? When they had this conversation, it was earlier this evening in front of Brett's house. But that can't be right. If it is from then, that can only mean one thing: Jabari was wearing a wire tonight! *Jabari was wearing a wire!* Edwyn's mouth slowly gapes open as he realizes what Jabari has done to him.

After all of these years, he was just looking for a perfect opportunity, laying low like a snake in the grass waiting to strike. Jabari was so angry at Edwyn for his father's death, rather than just take it and move on, he waited for the perfect opportunity to take revenge on Edwyn. But Jabari wanted to make sure whatever he did, Edwyn wouldn't recover from anytime soon. He always knew what Edwyn had done and that it was only a matter of time before he would think he could try to get Jabari Jr. involved in his criminal schemes. Maybe he thought Jabari had forgotten, or maybe he had remembered but wasn't angry anymore because he never mentioned his father. But the reality is, Jabari Jr. never forgot and was waiting for his one shot to get back at Edwyn. That opportunity presented itself, and he took full advantage. The new questions are, How did he do this? Who helped him? How long did it take for him to plan this?

Edwyn is so deep in thought that he doesn't even hear the question Gorman has posed. Gorman, upset, bangs on the table, startling Edwyn back to his senses.

"What?" Edwyn screams.

"I said," Gorman says with his voice rising, "let me get this straight: you threatened to fire Jabari if he didn't rob the Kinney house. When he still refused, you robbed it on your own and got caught. Now you are telling us it was Jabari who forced *you* to rob the house? I can only imagine you used the same tactics to get Jabari Sr. to commit various crimes over the years. It was one of those crimes that ultimately got him killed. Isn't that right?"

Edwyn has been outsmarted and is currently outnumbered. He feels the best thing to say is nothing until his reinforcements arrive. Then he will let the lawyers do the talking. Maybe they can come up with a strategy to even the score. As he's thinking about this, he's wringing his hands as if he wants to pull the skin off. Finally, he says in a weak voice, "I-I-Look, I'm not saying another word until I speak to my lawyer. I mean, I'm not saying anything until my lawyer gets here."

Clark stands up and says, "That's the smartest thing you've said so far."

Clark stands him up and starts to put the handcuffs back on him, but Gorman waves him off, thinking it won't be necessary. Handcuffs are generally reserved for violent criminals. Edwyn is a lot of things: charming, arrogant, and a little obtuse, but one thing he is not is violent.

⋏

Gorman leads the two detectives as they escort Edwyn out the door and down the hallway. There, Edwyn sees Jabari, his wife, and Jabari's lawyer, Seth Greenberg. Seth is a serious-looking man in a sharp suit. What Edwyn finds most shocking is Jabari himself. He looks almost confused as to why he's there. Edwyn also notices the way he's dressed: blue jeans, wheat-colored boots, and a white turtleneck sweater. What Edwyn doesn't see is any black. Not a stitch of black clothing is on him. Edwyn looks behind them and all around, wondering, hoping, and now praying that Katherine got the message and is there with the lawyers. But it's to no avail, and this whole situation has made Edwyn very confused and angry to the point where he barks out, "What the fuck is going on here?"

Jabari takes half a step in his direction and responds with, "I might ask you the same question. You told them I forced you to do a robbery?"

"You were in the house!" Edwyn says. "You were there. Tell them the truth."

At this moment Seth stands in front of Jabari, protecting him from Edwyn and also from possibly saying anything he will regret later.

"He did. Did you? Did you really think your clandestine operation was going to stay that way?" Seth says in his deep and commanding voice. Seth was always told he had a voice for radio. When he speaks, most people stop to see who is speaking and then focus on what he's talking about. That is probably one of the reasons Seth decided to become a lawyer. When he speaks, everyone within the immediate vicinity stops what they have been doing and looks at Seth. He commands people's presence, and he senses it.

Jabari does too. That is why Jabari now puts a gentle hand on Seth's shoulder and walks past him toward Edwyn and says, "You remember my lawyer, Seth, right?"

Edwyn now remembers when he asked Jabari the name of the lawyer he used in the murder case, and Jabari claimed he couldn't remember.

Seth puts his hand on Jabari's shoulder, gently pulling him back as he steps forward now that he's been given a proper introduction. He takes out a small notebook. The kind of notebook kids in middle school would use for English composition homework. The book itself looks worn, and almost every page has been written on. Seth takes half a step toward Edwyn and says, "This book belongs to Jabari Sr., and in it, he detailed all of your illegal and illicit activities. He gave me this book upon his death with explicit instructions not to use it against you unless you tried to involve his son, Jabari Jr. Now that you have tried to force my client to commit a robbery, as well as finally admitted to your role in Jabari Sr.'s death, he will sue you and the club."

Edwyn looks taken aback, but the last statement and his widening eyes show his surprise and almost annoyance.

"The club?" Edwyn repeats, making sure he heard correctly.

"Jabari Jr. has been subjected to racial discrimination for quite some time now in the form of comments, taunts, and so-called pranks, such as employees hanging nooses on his locker. Between those incidents and this recent fiasco of you trying to railroad my client into acts of criminality, by the time all is said and done, he will own you and the club," Seth says with cool certainty.

Jabari then turns to Edwyn, smiles slightly, and says, "I've made a very wise investment."

Edwyn is very miffed that Jabari has thrown his own line back in his face.

Seth doesn't want to give Edwyn a chance to ask any questions, so he moves toward Gorman and says, "Will that be all? My client is eager to get home."

Gorman moves closer to Edwyn and Jabari, extends his hand to them, and says, "Yes. And, Mr. Douglas, I am very sorry for any inconvenience this may have caused you or your wife."

Jabari grabs Gorman's hand and gives him a very hearty handshake and says, "It's quite all right, Sergeant. I'm just glad we got this all straightened out."

Edwyn looks on, almost jealous at the handshake, trying to remember the last time they shook hands.

⋏

Edwyn doesn't concentrate too long on that because Brett and Arlene are now walking into the station escorted by two police officers. Arlene, Brett, Sabriah, and Jabari greet the others with shared confusion, and they engage in small talk. Brett sees Edwyn out of the corner of his eye and is only thinking of one thing: rage, 100 percent pure, unadulterated rage. This was a man who hired and helped him to learn the ropes of the financial world. He considered Edwyn a good, close personal friend. All he remembers is Arlene picking him up off the floor and her screaming about how Edwyn had tried to rob their house. That image alone fills Brett with so much rage, he marches over to Edwyn.

"Look, let me explain," Edwyn says. Now he notices Brett's bandaged hand. "What happened to your hand?" Edwyn says without thinking.

Pow! Brett punches him so hard that he actually lifts Edwyn off his feet. If it weren't for the police behind him to catch him, Edwyn would have hit the ground hard. The police stand him up as Gorman and Clark hold Brett back from taking another shot. Seth, Sabriah, and Jabari watch the action from a safe distance, and Jabari mumbles loudly enough for the other two to hear, "I hope he washes his hands when he gets a chance."

Sabriah nudges him, letting him know this isn't the right time to make comments like that.

"After what I did for you, this is how you repay me?" Brett yells.

"After you did what? Stab me in the fucking back?" Edwyn retorts.

"I did not get you fired!" Brett says. Edwyn almost recoils back at that dreaded word. "It was George! It was always George!" Brett continues.

"George? How?" Edwyn says, clearly confused.

"For years, you were making all of those stupid-ass mistakes. Those mistakes added up and were costing the firm money. George made the recommendation to have you fired. Not me. It was never me."

Edwyn thinks about this for a minute and realizes it doesn't make any sense. "I just had dinner with George earlier tonight, and he all but guaranteed my job back. Why would he go to all that trouble to bring me back?" Edwyn asks.

"Trust me. If George is bringing you back, it's not because he wants to. He's probably being force to do it," Brett says with assurance.

Edwyn now looks very confused. He asks, "What do you mean forced? Like someone in upper management?"

Brett half laughs and says, "Don't be so fucking naive. Upper management was happy to see you go."

"Who, then? Who would have that kind of influence over him to make him try so hard?"

"My guess would be someone with a pussy." Brett delivers the line with such venom in his voice, the whole room stops whatever it was doing and looks at him. Brett is not known for his vulgarity, but the few times he does say something, he certainly catches everyone's attention.

Brett realizes there are several women in the room, including his wife, and is now slightly embarrassed. He looks around at the women and says, "Excuse me, ladies. I'm trying to make a point." He then turns back to Edwyn and says, "George is very much like you. He prides himself on his sexual conquests. Just like you. But he's no Bill Clinton. And neither are you."

And with that line, Arlene sheepishly looks at the ground, hoping no one sees her. Thankfully, no one does. Edwyn is too preoccupied to think about his history with Arlene.

"Look who's stupid now," Edwyn says, "There are no women in upper management."

Brett then takes a few steps closer to him. Officers move in just to make sure he doesn't hit Edwyn again. "I was actually referring to someone's wife," Brett says, hoping Edwyn will understand.

Edwyn says, "Oh, yeah? Whose wife would be so bold?" It should be known that at this point, everyone in the room has figured out Brett is referring to Katherine—everyone except Edwyn, of course, who is still fuming at the possibility that George was forced to give him his old job back.

And then it hits him. It can't be! Katherine was behind this? She forced George to get me my old job back?

Brett sees Edwyn's face and knows he has finally put the pieces together. "Look who finally paid the light bill!" Brett says, his voice dripping with sarcasm.

Now embarrassed and overcome with rage, Edwyn tries to rush Brett but is held back by the police.

"Let him go," Brett says. "It'll give me the satisfaction of knocking him down again."

"Fuck you!" Edwyn says, mainly because he has nothing better to say.

Brett now takes a step back from Edwyn and says, "Katherine. Fuck Katherine, which I'm sure is something George did in order for you to get your job back with the firm. You said it yourself and to me years ago. Katherine was only good at one thing."

Looking at the situation and seeing it get more awkward, Seth, Jabari, and Sabriah see no real need to be there. So they decide to make a quick exit. "Well, detectives, I think we've seen enough. If that's all, my client and I will be going now," Seth says as the three of them head out the door and into the parking lot.

Edwyn is now left standing there, still in police custody, still very confused, and still wondering where the fuck Katherine is. He was given one phone call, which he used to call the house hours ago. She was supposed to be home. She never mentioned she was going out. Edwyn is left wondering, what happens now?

CHAPTER 11

Outside in the parking lot, Seth, Jabari, and Sabriah say very little to one another as they head toward Seth's car. Once they reach the car, they all give one another knowing looks. Sabriah then leans forward a little and says in a gentle whisper, "It really work—" Before she can finish, Seth shushes her, and Jabari motions for her to just get in the car. They drive off the police parking lot and onto the street in silence. Seth is driving, Jabari is riding shotgun, and Sabriah is in the backseat looking at the two of them, wondering when she can speak about what she knows.

After a few agonizing moments, Seth and Jabari look at each other and nod knowingly. Seth glances back at Sabriah and says, "We have to be careful and not reveal too much—at least not so close to the police, where one of them could hear us."

Jabari then says, "We did it, didn't we?"

Seth smiles at his old friend and says, "Welcome to the club."

Sabriah then looks out the window and says, "I'm just glad things worked out the way they did."

Jabari, looking straight ahead, says, "Me too."

⚔

My father always said justice will come. It might not be today and it might not be tomorrow, but it will come in one way or another. You just have to be patient and wait for it. But when the opportunity arrives, don't hesitate.

In fact, the very last thing he said to me was, "Jabari, watch Edwyn. He'll slip up. He always does." Which is why back at my house, I walked in, still stunned by what Edwyn had said. I didn't even notice my wife, Sabriah, had rearranged the furniture again. Ever since we moved to our current apartment three years ago, she has been watching home décor shows religiously to get new ideas on how to position the furniture. Considering she is only five feet five and about 110 pounds, the fact she was able to move a couch; two chairs, one leather and one fabric; a coffee table; two lamps; and a wall unit is quite impressive.

She was standing with her back to me as she used a wall to stretch. She turned around to see me and at first didn't notice my mood or face. She moved over to the side so I could get a better look at all the furniture she had moved around.

"What do you think? I figured if we move the couch to this side, there would be more room in the center of the room. Good idea? I know you think I watch the home-decor channel too much, right?" She finally noticed my face and moved toward me. She dropped her smile and got dead serious. "What happened?"

I slowly looked at her and sighed deeply. "I think Edwyn wants me to commit a robbery," I finally said.

Sabriah forgot about the furniture completely and focused all of her attention on me. "He's trying to do to you what he did to your father?" she said.

"I think so," I said. With that, I went to the phone.

As I picked up the receiver, Sabriah said, "We need to call Seth. You remember the number, right?" I completely ignored and answered her question at the same time by dialing the number to his law firm, which I knew by heart. I even remembered the name of the receptionist there.

"Gibbons, Rose, and Cobb," said Shelia.

"Seth Rosenberg, please," I said.

"Mr. Rosenberg is with a client," Shelia said.

"Shelia, tell him it's Jabari Douglas Jr."

"I understand that, Mr. Douglas, but—"

"No!" I barked back. "You tell him I'm on the phone. You tell him, the conversation we always knew would happen has just happened. If he still doesn't want to talk to me, then I'll call back."

"Please hold," Shelia said.

After several agonizing moments, I heard the phone click over, and then I heard Seth's voice. "Jar Jar," Seth said as a *Star Wars* reference.

"Sith Lord," I said, a *Star Wars* reference of my own. "If we want him, we have to move fast."

"Get in my office now," Seth said.

▲

On the night I was going to put my plan into action, I was at Seth's office. I had my shirt off as Seth was helping put a wire on me. Sabriah was sitting behind the desk, very nervous about what was about to happen. Just as he had almost finished putting on the wire, Seth stood up to inspect its placement. "This might not be enough," he said to us.

Sabriah said, "You mean getting him on tape? How is that possible?"

"Like hell it won't," I said defiantly. I refused to believe all of this work would be for nothing. "So even if I get him to admit he wants to rob a house, you're saying that won't be enough? That's bullshit, and I refuse to believe it."

Seth sat back down and shook his head, telling me it wouldn't be enough. As soon as I finished my rant, Seth said, "Think for a minute. Even if you get him to admit everything, what then? You think they'll arrest him based on a taped confession? That's not how this works. You need hard evidence or some kind of definitive proof. Besides, Edwyn has been donating money to the police department in this county for years. You think he did that for no reason? Those donations are insurance that justice goes his way. Also, most of the judges and high-powered attorneys are members of the club, and he sees these people on a regular basis. We will be going up against an onslaught of powerful players who are not above breaking the law by bribing witnesses or paying to have key evidence removed to ensure a verdict in their favor. And for some of these people, all they have to do is make one phone call. That's part of the appeal of joining the club. You have unlimited access to the very powerful, and that's the kind of power that money can't buy."

Sabriah asked, "Have you applied to be a member of the club?"

Seth and I both looked at each other and then looked at her.

"That club has three nos. No blacks," Seth said.

"No Jews," I chimed in.

"And no gays," Seth said, finishing it off. Seth and I have known each other for a very long time and have a wonderful rapport where we can riff with each other right on cue.

Seth said, "Will Samson, who was a longtime member of the club and was charged with double murder, called my father to defend him because he heard how good my father was. My father picked apart the prosecutor's case bit by bit, and his closing argument, 'Reasonable Doubt versus Unreasonable Doubt,' was so good, law schools still analyze it. After all was said and done, Will thanked my father with a hearty handshake, paid his legal fees in full, and then promptly denied my father's existence. My father left message after message but got nowhere. He was one of the most successful lawyers in Westchester County and had just won a seemingly unwinnable case. My father had a great career, home, and family. But what he wanted most of all was to be one of the boys, a place to belong and hang out. And they denied him because he was a Jew. Can you fucking believe that? Trust me, no one wants to get this asshole more than I do, but we need more."

I mulled the options over in my head and sat down next to Seth. After a few minutes, I said, "What if he got arrested?"

"Arrested where?" Seth asked.

"In Brett's house," I replied.

"How would he get in the house?" Seth asked again.

I wasn't really interested in hearing the roadblocks to the problem. I banged the desk in frustration and said, "I'm just talking hypothetical. Put down your legal cap for a second and answer the question."

Seth paused for a moment and then said, "Well, in that case, he'd be finished. With the real prospect of jail, most of his friends would abandon him, and he would lose almost all of his influence. How would you get him in the house, anyway?"

I was rubbing my face and didn't answer him. Seth and Sabriah glanced at each other, wondering about my silence. They looked at my brooding face for a moment until he came to sit next to me and said, "We're not talking hypothetical, are we?" I just stared ahead. "Listen, Jar," Seth began. "We need to be together on this." I still said nothing, so Seth went to his desk and pulled out a small, worn notebook.

As soon as I saw it, my eyes lit up. I recognized it right away. "Hey, that was my dad's," I said, pointing to it.

"I know," Seth replied. "He gave it to me before he died."

"I always saw him writing in it, but he never let me see inside," I said.

Now that he finally had my attention, he again asked, "How will you get him in the house? Because based on how that goes, we can incorporate this."

"It's easy when you deal with those people," I said sarcastically.

"Those people?" Seth asked with a smirk.

"You're talking about a man who, if you're not in the same tax bracket as he is, doesn't give you a second glance. This is a man who will take a piss or a shit and won't even look at the sink because he literally thinks his shit don't stink. I saw him do that once, and I never shook his hand again. Edwyn prides himself on two things: money and status. They go hand in hand, and he hasn't had much of one and is losing a lot of the other. Edwyn has been out of work for over a year, and he still blames Brett for that. He wants revenge," I said with confidence.

"And?" Seth asked, prodding me to continue.

I looked Seth directly in the eye and said, "And Edwyn's not that bright. He never was. I've known him for years. I know all of his wants and desires. He wants money and desires power. Trust me. I can get him in the house. I will get him in the house."

Seth and I stared at each other and had a conversation without words. After a few minutes, Seth moved closer to me with the notebook and said, "After he's arrested, we'll use this to really nail him."

"Let me see it," I said with great anticipation, finally getting a chance to see what was in my father's book. And with that, Seth opened it up.

⚔

Edwyn was sitting in the car looking embarrassed because he didn't know what indignation meant. He slowly lowered his hand, knowing that I would never shake it. I stared at his face, his hand, and then back at his face, and then I finally exited the car and headed toward the house.

As soon as I was out of Edwyn's line of sight, I took off my backpack, removed my hat, and took out a very realistic Bill Clinton latex mask. I had looked all over the city and found a great shop downtown that sold real masks for every occasion. I put the mask and my hat back on and then took out the two-way radio I would use to speak to Edwyn. I then took out another two-way radio. This one had red hearts drawn all over it.

"You there?" I asked in a whisper.

Around the corner from where Edwyn was parked, Seth and Sabriah sat in Seth's car. They had arrived about an hour before Edwyn and I did. Since the engine and lights were off, it was quite chilly. They both were sharing a blanket that was in the backseat. They also sat in a reclining position so no passersby would see them, but, as is true in most suburban areas after a certain hour, very few people are actually on the street. Seth took out the other two-way radio, which also had hearts drawn on it.

"We're just around the corner. You in the house yet?" Seth asked, also in a whisper.

"Just about. Give me thirty seconds," I said.

"Remember what we talked about," Seth said very nervously. "Get in. More importantly, get him in as quickly as you can and get out."

I looked around, making sure no one was around as I said, "I got it."

It was at this moment that Sabriah snatched the radio out of Seth's hands and sat up. Her voice quivered with fear, expressing nervousness and apprehension. She realized this situation could go very wrong very quickly. She didn't want me to get caught and go to jail. That was something no one really wanted. Seth told me later that tears formed around her eyes when she said, "Jabari Hasani Douglas Jr." She wasn't trying to hide her emotions from me because she wanted to me to know exactly how she felt. And I did. And I wanted to let her know that while this was a gamble and there was the real prospect of me getting arrested, I had complete faith in the plan Seth and I had laid down. The possibility of finally getting the man who had my father killed was well worth the risk of entrapping him in the Kinney house.

I said, "Sabriah Mas'ouda Douglas." I also said this in almost a normal voice. I then turned off the radio and headed to the Kinney house. I slowly turned the knob to the back door and was surprised to find it unlocked. I shook my head and remembered when Edwyn told me they didn't lock their back door because everyone in this area felt safe. I opened the door just enough to slip inside—making only the slightest noise.

$$\blacktriangle$$

I stayed low to the ground and headed toward the huge island in the kitchen. In the background, I heard the television and then footsteps. Whoever it was, was heading in my direction, so I moved closer to the island for cover. Arlene, in a bit of a daze, walked in with her empty wine glass and opened the fridge to see if there was anything for her to snack on, but to no avail. She closed the door and went to refill her wine glass. As she was about to pour, I snuck up behind her and put her in a choke hold. She dropped the bottle immediately to try to break my grasp, but the choke was so tight, she couldn't. Arlene couldn't do much of anything except muster semiloud grunts. I leaned back, lifting her off the ground for more potency, and Arlene was rendered unconscious. I then very gingerly picked her up, carried her back to the living room, and gently placed her in the chair.

All of a sudden, I heard Brett's voice. "Honey, what was that? You OK?" he said from the den. He had obviously heard the bottle shatter before she went unconscious. I just stood there, waiting for him to show and thinking what to do. "Arlene?" Brett said again, and I heard his footsteps coming closer. A few moments later, Brett emerged from the den and was scared stiff. An intruder was in his house!

"What the fuck are you doing in my house?" Brett demanded. From where he stood in the back of the house, with no lights on, he saw a white male wearing all black and a black hat with white or gray hair coming out of the sides. Brett was trying to remember the individual's face so he could tell the police later.

Brett took a step closer and said again, "I said, what the fuck—"

Suddenly I pretended I was charging him, just to get him to run away. And he did, right back into the den. I took this opportunity to run upstairs and hide. Brett, though, opened his gun cabinet, which housed his impressive gun collection. The guns were locked behind glass doors so he and others could admire them. It opened with a special key that Brett was now very desperate to look for. Since he couldn't find it, and because he heard me run upstairs, he broke the glass with his hand and pulled out a double-barrel shotgun. He also grabbed a box of shells and threw them on a nearby work desk to load the gun.

With the gun now loaded, he went to look for the intruder. Brett, whose hand was dripping blood everywhere, slowly moved back to the living room, where he had first seen me. He went to Arlene and checked her pulse to make sure she was still alive. Assured she was unconscious but otherwise unharmed, he then moved toward the staircase. To get a better view of the upstairs, Brett used his bloody hand to lean against the wall as he went upstairs, streaking the walls with blood.

At the top of the stairs, Brett stood and stared down a long hallway. With the doors on both sides being either bedrooms or closets, it was hard for him to figure out where I was. Some doors were open, and some were closed. He decided to search the first bedroom and move forward down the hall from there. He did a quick scan of the room—a modest-sized bed and a full, freestanding armoire near the window. He looked under the bed and in the closet. Those were the most obvious spots.

He walked out of the room and went to the next one. He thought he shut the door with enough force for it to close all the way, but it only closed slightly. Not wanting to go back to shut it, he moved on to another room. What he didn't know was, I was hiding on the other side of the armoire!

I quietly opened the door and snuck up behind Brett and gave him a vicious, hard choke hold. As soon as Brett felt those arms around his neck, he dropped the gun and tried to break free. Unlike the shorter Arlene, whom I had to lift off the floor for leverage in the choke, I bent down with him. Not only did I bend down, I also moved back at the same time, preventing Brett from getting his footing and taking away his leverage, and choked him out in a few minutes.

As I let Brett fall gently to the floor, I took out the two-way radio I used with Edwyn and figured out a way to get him to come in the house.

"You there?" I said in a very faint whisper, trying to stifle my breathing.

"Yeah. You coming out soon? This is taking too long," Edwyn said, also in a whisper. I heard the nervousness in his voice and used that as a catalyst.

"You weren't kidding when you said this guy was loaded. There's millions here," I said matter-of-factly.

"Millions?"

I could tell from the tone in his voice that he was very excited about hearing that, so I said, "Cash, jewelry, and gold."

"Gold?" Edwyn said.

BINGO!

"Yeah. There's at least ten gold bars up here. But there's no way I can carry all this by myself. You have to help me," I told him.

There was a slight pause on the phone, and I sensed some apprehension. "I can't," he said, with direct concern for his own safety.

That wasn't going to work at all for me. Edwyn had to come in the house, but I couldn't make it sound like I was too desperate; otherwise, Edwyn would suspect something. He's not that stupid. I decided to play it cool with the best closing line ever. "That's fine. We'll have to abort for now and come back another time and figure out how we can carry all of this stuff, because I can't do it alone. I'll be out in five minutes," I said finally.

"No!" Edwyn shouted, before catching himself and lowering his voice. "I-I'll be up in a minute."

"No. Now. The clock is ticking." I then turned off my radio before Edwyn could respond. I grabbed the two-way for Seth and my wife. "Where is he? Is he in the house yet?" I asked.

Seth picked up the radio and said, "Hang on a sec." He handed the radio to Sabriah as he quietly got out of the car and skulked around the corner to get a look at Edwyn still sitting in the car, looking down at the lap before finally getting out. Edwyn stood there beside the car for a few minutes before going toward the back of the house. Seth turned to Sabriah and nodded.

"He's on his way in the house," Sabriah said in the two-way.

I went into the master bedroom to where the safe was, and, by using the combination Edwyn had given me, I was able to open it. I then hid in the doorway of the bedroom next to the master bedroom, waiting for Edwyn. I heard him come up the stairs and ducked farther into the bedroom, out of sight.

"We have to make the call, you know," Seth said to Sabriah.

She nodded knowingly but was still very worried.

Seth put his hand on hers and tried to reassure her. "He'll be fine. He'll get out in time. He has to," Seth said to her again with a gentle tone in his voice.

Seth took out a prepaid phone he had brought with him. It was the kind of phone people buy when they can't afford to sign on with a legit carrier. They're cheap, disposable, and, most of the time, very hard to trace. Seth took a deep breath, dialed 911, and said, "Yes, hello? I'd like to report a break-in…"

⅄

I heard Edwyn breathing a sigh of relief after nudging Brett's body to make sure he was still alive. I then heard Edwyn moving around in the next room. I heard Sabriah say in a faint voice, "Cops'll be here soon. Hurry."

I had to get out of the house, but before I did, I needed to grab that other two-way. As I was thinking about how to get the radio from Edwyn, I looked around the room to find out how to get out of the house. The bedroom window was open a crack, which was all the window of opportunity I needed. I glanced over to see if the coast was clear and saw a woman in the next house hanging out of her bedroom window smoking a cigarette. Shit! This was the last thing I needed. Now I had to grab the radio and get out of the house without being seen.

"Where the fuck is the rest? Where's the gold?" I heard Edwyn say. I heard the confusion and slight notes of anger and fear in his voice. I wanted to see exactly where he was, so I stuck my head out of the bedroom I was hiding in to take a peek. At that moment, Edwyn stuck his head out the door, looking for me. Luckily, I pulled my head back in just in time. He would have seen me if he had looked in my direction first.

Then I heard Edwyn start to fill the bag up with valuables from the safe. I glanced next door to see if the woman was still smoking and saw that she was gone. The coast was clear, but I still couldn't leave without that radio. Then I heard something hit the floor, followed by Edwyn yelling, "Shit!" Curious, I snuck up to the bedroom doorway, poked my head in for a second, and saw it was the radio that had fallen. It actually very close to the door, so I wouldn't reach very far to grab it. I hid again in the room and then took another quick look. Seeing that Edwyn was very distracted, I quickly reached in and grabbed the radio.

Right away, I went back to the other bedroom, saw the coast was still clear, and quietly opened the window enough to slide through to the outside. I remembered to put the window back at the same level afterward. Because I was only on the second level and wore shoes with good grips on the bottoms, I climbed out of the windows and onto one of the dormers. From the dormer to the eave was pretty steep. I had to press my back against the field of the roof and use my full weight to keep from falling off. Once I got to the eave, I looked down and saw it was too high to jump, so I had to hang from the edge and jump down into the backyard. I walked around to the street where Seth and Sabriah were waiting for me. I heard the faint sound of police sirens in the background.

I lightly tapped on the window of Seth's car. Sabriah and Seth were startled, and Sabriah got out, opened the back door, and slid in. As soon as I was in the car, I took the mask off, and Seth started the engine.

The sound of the police sirens grew louder and louder, and soon there was a police car crossing the intersection directly in front of us. We must have waited about thirty seconds and then slowly moved the car straight down the street, passing the intersection. As we were driving, I saw the police put the handcuffs on Edwyn. "Slow down. Slow down," I said, almost begging Seth.

Seth slowed down and said, "We really shouldn't linger." But now, seeing Edwyn looking in the direction of our car, not knowing who we were, and turning away in embarrassment brought on a wealth of emotion. I was remembering how he had treated my father and made him do things, how he would call the house at all hours of the night and make my father get dressed to run errands for him. Seeing him in this position brought tears in my eyes.

I said, "I've waited a long time to see this." Sabriah touched my face lightly. After watching the police place handcuffs on Edwyn and lead him in the patrol car, I said, "We can go now."

Seth started to go faster, and then we all put our game faces on.

"What happens now?" Sabriah asked.

I started to take off my shirt, revealing the wire I was wearing, and said, "I got it all. He admitted to getting Dad killed."

Seth slapped the steering wheel and said, "Excellent! Give that to me so I can loop it on with the other recordings I have. Now, one thing I know about those people is they always fold under questioning, especially when their backs are up against the wall."

"Those people?" I said with a smile.

Seth only glanced at me, knowing full well what I was referring to. "He has enough clout to at least get the police to bring you down to the station for questioning. Expect them, but act surprised. They will try to pressure you to make incriminating statements. Don't say anything until I get there. That's very important," he said.

I continued to take off all of my clothes and put them in a bag Sabriah and I had brought with us. "We need to burn the clothes, the mask, everything," I said.

"My wife's already got the fireplace going strong as we speak. Give everything to me," Seth said with a wink and a grin.

"We've got him by the balls, don't we?" Sabriah said.

Seth and I looked at each other and slightly smiled. "Yup," Seth said. "I've got one..."

"...and I've got the other," I said.

"As soon as they take him out of the house, Sabriah, call me right away. I'll come get you, and we'll go to the station together," Seth told her in exacting fashion. "In the meantime, you guys get ready."

I grabbed my wife's hand and said, "We'll be ready."

⅄

Back at our house, the dinner table looked as if it belonged at a five-star restaurant. There were wonderfully placed tablecloths, napkins, plates, silverware, and wine glasses. Those home-improvement channels my wife watches really come in handy! For food, there was garlic-flavored mashed potatoes, broccoli rabe, lamb chops, and a just-opened bottle of Italian wine.

But eating was not on the menu at the moment. Sabriah and I sat on the couch watching HGTV, just waiting for the police to arrive. We both seemed oddly calm, considering what had happened already. I turned to my wife and said, "Look, when these cops come, we have to make it look good. They can't know we know anything. We have to be as convincing as possible if this is going to work, OK?"

⅄

Then we heard the hard knock on the door, and we knew it could only be the police. Most people ring the bell once or even twice before resorting to knocking on the door, but even then, the knock is a normal one. This was more of a bang to let you know they were serious. Sabriah and I moved quickly and quietly; Sabriah poured the wine as I put food on the plates.

"One second, please," I yelled in the direction of the door. Once everything was set, I went to answer the door, and, just as I thought, there were two plainclothes officers. They looked so serious; they could have only been police officers.

"Jabari Douglas?" said one of the officers.

"Jabari Douglas Jr.," I corrected them.

"I'm Officer Geno, and this is Officer Burnowski. Do you know a man named Edwyn Collingsworth?"

"I'm sorry, but can I see some ID, please?" I said to them. They both took out their police credentials and presented them. Once I looked them over, I was satisfied they were the real deal. I said, "Yes. I do know him. How can I help you, gentlemen?"

"There's a situation downtown, and we need to have you come with us to answer a few questions," Officer Geno said again. The other officer just stood there, not really saying much. He looked almost like a trainee learning the ropes on how to question someone at his or her house.

"Come with you for what? Can you tell me what this is in regard to?"

"This is kind of a sensitive matter, and we just need to ask you a few routine questions," the officer replied.

"Just a few routine questions," Officer Burnowski said.

The first officer and I looked almost surprised when he spoke.

At this point Sabriah came to the door, looking very confused and very worried. "Honey?" she said. "What's this? What's going on?"

"Apparently there's a situation with Edwyn at the police station, and the officers need me to come with them," I told her.

"Oh, he's probably drunk again. Was he naked this time?" Sabriah said with a smile, not looking too worried.

But I looked at the officers and saw the seriousness in their faces. "I don't think so," I said to my wife, while still looking at the officers.

Sabriah now looked more serious and said, "What could this be about?"

I took a deep breath and said, "I'm not sure, but I hope Edwyn didn't do what he said he was going to do."

Both officers looked at each other strangely and then back at Sabriah and me. We both refrained from looking at each other, but with that, Sabriah and I knew that Seth was right. Edwyn had spilled the beans, and he had enough pull to get the cops to come to my house and bring me to the station.

"How long do you think this will take?" Sabriah asked with more worry.

"Ma'am, I have no idea," Officer Geno said.

Sabriah stepped a little closer to the doorway and said, "Well, what does that mean? You come to my home and take my husband to the station for questioning about a 'sensitive' situation, and when he asks how long this will take, you say 'I have no idea'?" The tears were slowly streaming down her face now and making the officers very uncomfortable. I was very surprised at her performance.

"Ma'am, I'm sure this is nothing to be worried about," Officer Geno said.

"I understand that, but if you knew Edwyn like we do, you wouldn't say that. Trust me—when it comes to him, nothing is as simple as it seems. I just don't want anything to happen to my husband." She then started crying heavily and collapsed in my arms.

I hugged her, rocked her back and forth, and said, "I promise I won't end up like my father."

Again, the officers looked at each other and then back at me and Sabriah.

I asked her to grab my sweater by the dresser. She went to do it, still crying, of course. The officers didn't really have much to say, mainly because they didn't really know what was going on. They were just cops doing what they were told.

Sabriah returned with my white turtleneck sweater. I put it on and said, "I shouldn't be long." We kissed, and she started bawling again as the officers and I left. She locked the doors and went to the window. As soon as she saw the officers put me in the car, she picked up the phone and called Seth.

"Seth, it's me," she said.

"What happened? They came for him? Did they take him?" Seth asked.

"They just left."

Seth noticed the tone in her voice and that she sounded upset. "Were you crying?" he asked, very concerned.

"What? Oh, yeah. I was," Sabriah said, now wiping her tears.

"But you knew they were coming. Why were you crying?" Seth asked.

"The crying was for them. No matter how rough, tough, and hard the cops are, they are no match for the raw power of a woman crying. Nothing can bring a man to his knees faster than a woman crying. The act was good enough for the cops to be fooled, and that's all that really mattered," Sabriah told Seth.

There was a pause on the other end until Seth finally said, "Good job. Get ready. I'll be there in fifteen minutes."

"I'll be ready," Sabriah said and then hung up the phone and poured herself a very generous glass of wine as a way to congratulate herself on her performance with the police. She sipped the wine and remarked to herself on how good it was. She looked at the bottle and said, "Wow. I have to write that one down." She continued to sip the wine while she waited for Seth.

$$\lambda$$

In the police interrogation room, I had been sitting in the same position for quite a while. I rarely looked up at Officers Clark and Johnson as they glanced at each other, trying to figure out a way to get me to talk. They were frustrated because time is always a factor with things like this. The longer I stayed quiet, the harder it would be for them to get me to talk.

"Look, we don't think you were involved," Clark said.

"We just want to know why Edwyn kept insisting we speak to you. Why would he do that?" Johnson added.

Now, Seth had told me not to say anything until he got there, but I was overwhelmed with curiosity. Knowing what had happened, I was very curious as to what Edwyn had told the police. So I sat up in my chair and said, "What did he tell you exactly?"

The officers were so excited I was talking, they both pulled up chairs to sit. Clark on one side, Johnson on the other.

"He said the whole thing was your idea," Clark said.

I then looked up from the table and stared Clark square in the eye. "He said that?" I asked.

"That's what I heard," Clark replied.

"That's what you heard, but were you listening?" I said very sternly.

Johnson moved his hands closer to me just to get my attention and said, "Is there a difference?"

"That depends. Do you know the difference between a cop and a detective?" I asked Clark.

Clark looked at Johnson, smiled slightly, and said, "At a crime scene, it's the cop's job to close off the area from traffic, be it pedestrian or motor. It's the detective's job to figure out what happened and look for clues. I've been a detective for six years."

I shifted a little in my chair and said, "That is correct. Do you know where I was when the cops picked me up?" I asked.

"They said you were home," Clark responded.

"Not only was I home," I said. "I was just about to have a late dinner with my wife."

Johnson leaned forward and said, "Why don't we go back—"

"Do you know where Edwyn was when the cops picked him up?" I asked, cutting Johnson off. Clark and Johnson looked at each other, wondering if they should tell me.

"That's not really relevant right now," Johnson said.

I knew I had them. I leaned back in my chair and said, "And there's your answer. If he were anywhere else but at home, you might have something. Case closed."

Clark and Johnson glanced at each other and then back at me, a little confused. "What do you mean, case closed? How is that closed?" Clark said, a bit annoyed.

I sat up and said, "You say you don't know, but I believe you do. I believe if he had been at home, you would have told me. In fact, you would have told me what he was doing. If he were eating, you would tell me what he was eating. If he were watching TV, you would tell me what program. The fact that you didn't tell me says you really don't know, or he wasn't at home. I think you really don't believe I had anything to do with this, but because Edwyn has donated so much money to this department, and to this building in particular, you are almost obligated to bring me down for what you call routine questioning."

Clark and Johnson looked shocked at my analysis. Observing this, I poured it on by saying, "Don't be shocked by what I'm saying. You guys even gave him a special police tag for the dashboard of his car, and I heard all about those times when he had one too many and you let him off with a warning. Now something big has come up, something so big that a warning just won't do and quick action has to be taken. I don't know where he was, and I don't care, but if he was anywhere but at home, that's not a good sign."

Johnson and Clark were amazed at how fast I put these pieces together.

I leaned back in the chair again and said, "I have nothing to hide. You know who does? Criminals."

At this point, Sergeant Gorman came in the room, followed by Seth. He too was dressed differently than he had been earlier in the evening.

"Gentlemen," Gorman began, "this is Seth Greenberg, Jabari's lawyer."

Both Clark and Johnson looked at each other and then at me.

"I told you there was no need for a lawyer because you haven't been charged with anything," Johnson said.

"Well, my client isn't concerned about answering questions. I'm here to make sure that when my client is ready to leave, he can do so freely instead of being questioned nonstop until he is broken to the point where he confesses to everything. I've seen you do that before to a client of mine," Seth said very matter-of-factly. All of the officers in the room now had nothing to say, mainly because what Seth said was 100 percent accurate.

Gorman said, "Mr. Greenberg was also the lawyer for Jabari Douglas Sr."

"That is correct. And for years, I represented Jabari Sr., who was not so much a criminal as he was a victim of a crime," Seth said.

Johnson took a step closer and said, "What crime was that?"

"Power," Seth said. "In order to gain leverage over prominent players in the financial services scene, Jabari Sr. was, many times, forced to dig dirt on the opposition. Sometimes, this would involve breaking into people's homes. One night he broke into the wrong house, and he was shot."

All grew quiet in the room, and Seth put a reassuring hand on my shoulder.

"Who forced him?" Johnson asked.

Seth nodded to Sergeant Gorman, who then placed a folder on the table, and Seth took a miniature tape recorder out of his pocket, placed it on the table, looked at everyone in the room, and said, "Listen to this." Seth then hit Play.

Chapter 12

By the time Katherine has walked all the way home, she feels as though she has run a marathon. Her feet feel as if they are in buckets of cement, and every step is agony. She wants badly to go back to her car, but she feels it is important to keep up the illusion that she is looking for her "husband." The police have, after all, killed Ernesto and arrested every prostitute in that house. She has no real choice.

Another option for her is to hop in a cab. Lord knows there have been many that honked at her, seeking a fare. Again, though, she decides against it because many cabs have video cameras recording everything, to prevent robberies.

She has to remain hidden. She looks up and sees the sky change from a charcoal gray to a light blue. The dawn is definitely breaking the skies overhead. When she walks into her house, she shuts the door without locking it and looks around.

"You here?" she bellows throughout the house. She looks around and realizes neither one of them has been home all night. Edwyn did mention he was going out to celebrate the dinner he had with George. Is he still out? Where could he be? For a minute, Katherine thinks that maybe he is out with some prostitute, which is fine as long as he doesn't bring home any sexual diseases such as herpes or gonorrhea.

Katherine slinks upstairs to the bedroom, where she peels off her clothes, takes the money Lailani has sewn in the lining of the coat, and counts it. In a short period of time, the girl had managed to stash almost $400. Katherine wonders how she was able to put away so much in such a short period of time. Was the money from tips, or did she steal it? In any event, it is Katherine's now, because possession is nine-tenths of the law. She lays the money on the bed, and now the only other thing on her mind at the moment is to hit the shower. She smells like the streets, and she wants nothing more than to wash off the funk of the night.

She uses almost no cold water as she tries to wash all of the events off of her body. It is one of the best showers she's had in a very long time.

Finally refreshed, she walks to the kitchen to make herself a cup of coffee. As the coffee is brewing, she happens to notice the answering machine is blinking, with three messages waiting. After a moment's hesitation, she hits Play. The first one is Eugenia's voice. She sounds tired and scared. Her message says, "Hi, Miss Collingsworth. This is Eugenia. I don't think I'll be coming in today. I just got a call from the police that my brother was shot and killed last night. I don't have all of the details, but they need me to come down and identify the body. I'm really scared, Miss C. I've been a loyal employee for you, and I hope if I ever needed your help, you would—"

Katherine deletes the rest of the message. After all that has happened, she really isn't interested in hearing from Eugenia. Besides, Katherine knows exactly what happened to her brother and why.

She moves on to the next message. It's Edwyn. He also sounds tired and scared. His message says, "Honey? It's me. You're not going to believe this, but I'm at the police station. Before you get angry, just know it wasn't my fault. I need you to come down here right away. Bring bail money, and you might want to call the lawyer. In fact, bring two lawyers. See if you can find the number to one of the lawyers at Seth Greenberg's firm. That asshole Jabari fucked me. Anyway, come down, and I'll explain."

She looks at the machine in disgust and looks away. "You fucking asshole!" Katherine rages. "I told you not to do anything stupid! Didn't I tell you that? Jackass!" The veins in her neck are bulging as she explodes at the machine.

The third and last message plays. This one is George, who sounds tired but relieved. His message is this: "Edwyn? It's George. Hey, buddy, listen, I have great news. You got your old job back. That's right! We want to bring you back on right away. But there's a catch. Actually, there are two catches. The first one is, we're still waiting for the final approval for a full-time hire. In the meantime, we have to bring you on as a consultant. The rate we're giving you is seventy-five dollars an hour. Isn't that great? I know it's not what you were making before, but it's just until we get the final sign-off. The second catch is, you need to call me to approve the rate. There's a very small window of opportunity to finalize this. You have five hours from this message to call me. I don't care where you are or what you're doing. Unless you're dead or in jail, you need to call me; otherwise, the deal is off. Those aren't my terms. This is coming from upper management. Hope to hear from you soon. Say hi to Katherine for me."

Katherine compares the time stamp from the last message to the time frame George gave and realizes the offer expires in ninety minutes.

She now fixes her cup of coffee and heads outside. She steps outside her door to watch the sun rise and breathes that fresh suburban air. Men walking their dogs glance at her a little too long. She is strikingly beautiful. She closes her eyes and lifts her head to the sky. She has a great life, a beautiful house, and an awesome body. She then opens her eyes and asks the question, "What do I do now?"

Made in the USA
Middletown, DE
23 August 2017